CASTA #1

Worst Class Trip Ever

By Sandy Beech
Illustrated by Jimmy Holder

Aladdin Paperbacks
New York   London   Toronto   Sydney

ALADDIN PAPERBACKS
An imprint of Simon & Schuster Children's Publishing Division
1230 Avenue of the Americas, New York, NY 10020
Text copyright © 2005 by Catherine Hapka
Illustrations copyright © 2005 by Jimmy Holder
All rights reserved, including the right of
reproduction in whole or in part in any form.
ALADDIN PAPERBACKS and colophon are registered
trademarks of Simon & Schuster, Inc.
Designed by Tom Daly
The text of this book was set in Golden Cockerel.
Manufactured in the United States of America
First Aladdin Paperbacks edition June 2005
2 4 6 8 10 9 7 5 3 1
Library of Congress Control Number 2004109005
ISBN 0-689-87596-7

**ne**

Did you ever have a moment that seemed totally unimportant at the time, but then later you realized it was the moment when your whole life changed? Watching my middle-school science teacher eat a barbecued bug was that moment for me.

But maybe I should start from the beginning. My name is Dani McFeeney. That's short for Danielle, but nobody ever calls me that except my little brother, Kenny, and he's totally obnoxious. But more on that later.

The story really starts with Mr. Truskey.

Thompson Q. Truskey is the craziest teacher at Tweedale

Middle School. He's probably the nuttiest teacher in the state of Florida, or possibly the whole US of A. Despite that, they still let him teach sixth- and seventh-grade science.

I was on my way to his classroom one day when my friend Cassie Saunders caught up to me. "Did you hear?" she cried breathlessly. Cassie is almost always breathless. It's pretty much how she and her identical twin sister, Chrissie, go through life.

"Did I hear what?" I asked distractedly, less focused on Cassie than on what kind of mystery meat the cafeteria might be serving for lunch that day. Judging from the smell wafting through the halls, it had to be something like water buffalo, or possibly emu.

Cassie fell into step beside me as we rounded the corner at the end of the hall. "I heard Truskey has some kind of big announcement today," she said, tugging at a strand of her curly, shiny black hair. "Not just big—like, *huge*."

I shrugged. "Yeah?" I said. "It's probably something like the time he liberated those earthworms we were supposed to dissect."

We both grimaced at the memory. Mr. Truskey isn't just a teacher, he's an environmental activist, too. During the summer he's always going on these exotic quests to

sample soil quality in the jungles of Outer Middle-of-Nowhere or to save the greater swamp-dwelling sludge frog. At the beginning of the year he spent about four class periods telling us all about how he single-handedly flew a propeller plane deep into the rain forest of Costa Rica and piloted a motorboat down the Amazon, though it's hard to believe he could do either of those things and return in one piece. I've seen him screeching out of the teachers' parking lot in his ancient hatchback, and it's not a pretty sight.

But back to the worms. The poor, doomed worms. Mr. Truskey "liberated" them by releasing them into the potted ficus tree in Principal Hall's office. Unfortunately he failed to notice that the ficus was fake. The janitor must have been peeling dried-up worms off the carpet for days. Even though it was pretty funny, I think a lot of kids felt a little sorry for Mr. Truskey after that one. He always means well, even if he's kind of a spaz.

When Cassie and I entered the classroom, Mr. Truskey was already at the front of the room, pacing. His wild black hair looked even wilder than usual, and he was wearing flip-flops and an I HEART BIODIVERSITY T-shirt.

"People!" he called, clapping his hands as the bell rang

and everyone scrambled for their seats. "Simmer down. Before we get back to our discussion on electricity, I have something very exciting to tell you."

"You're getting a haircut?" Ryan Rodriguez called out from his seat in the back row. Ryan is the ADHD-fueled class clown of the sixth grade. He's physically unable to sit still for more than 4.3 seconds at a time and drives most of the teachers crazy.

Mr. Truskey leaned back against the front of his desk and smiled patiently as everyone snickered. "Sorry to disappoint you, Ryan," he said. "But it's almost as exciting as that. Ms. Watson and I just finished a meeting with Principal Hall. He's approved my proposal for a special trip to the Esparcir Islands!"

For a second we all thought he was talking about his next summer adventure. I guess we looked underwhelmed, because Mr. Truskey's eyes opened even wider as he stood up and jumped on top of his desk, sending papers and pencils flying.

"People! Did you hear me?" he exclaimed, flinging his arms wide, tripping on a stapler, and almost toppling himself back onto the floor. "Ten of you are going to have the adventure of a lifetime! You'll get to come with me,

see a part of the world few have ever seen, and help save the planet!"

Pacing back and forth, his flip-flops flapping against the Formica desktop, he explained the rest. Ten students from Tweedale Middle School—sixth, seventh, and eighth graders—would be spending five days on a tiny island near the equator that was supposed to be the habitat of a bunch of rare species. There the students would be cleaning up an old trash dump so the whole island could be turned into a wildlife refuge. Some rich guy in our town had already donated a bunch of money to cover all the major expenses, which meant all the students had to pay for was sunscreen and souvenirs. Best of all, the trip would take place in just three weeks. Anyone who went would get full science class credit for the time they were gone, and would have plenty of extra time to make up any work they missed in their other classes.

As Mr. Truskey blabbed on and on about the glorious wildlife of the Espa-whatever island chain, Cassie leaned over from her seat across the aisle. "Whoa!" she whispered. "A trip to the islands that counts as school? How cool is that?"

I had to admit it was pretty darn cool. As the rest of the

class murmured at the news, I raised my hand. "Mr. Truskey? Totally awesome idea! And the wildlife refuge sounds like a great cause. Sign me up!"

I could already imagine it: me and my two best friends, Michelle and Tina, setting off on our island adventure. The three of us would work together in the balmy island breeze, picking up old tin cans and whatnot in a beautiful palm grove. Later we would lounge on the beach, feeling good about our day's work. Talk about perfect! We could save the world and get a tan at the same time.

Mr. Truskey seemed pleased at my enthusiasm. "Groovy, Dani," he said. "I'll hang a sign-up sheet on the bulletin board outside. Just get permission from your parents first."

"I will," I promised, visions of body surfing on crystal clear Caribbean waters dancing in my head. "I'll call them right after class."

After that, things happened fast. Sort of like a train wreck.

As soon as I left Mr. Truskey's class, I rushed to the office to call my parents, cursing the annoying Tweedale Middle School rule that bans students from carrying cell phones during school hours. When I reached my mom

at the newspaper where she works, she sounded surprised as I blurted out the whole story.

"Are you sure this is something you're interested in,
Dani?" she asked. "It sounds like it could involve some
hard work."

"I'm up for it, Mom, I swear," I told her. "Love me some
environmental causes—you know that."

She was silent for a second. I crossed my fingers, press-
ing the phone to my ear and listening to the muffled
hustle and bustle of the newspaper office in the background.

"All right, Dani," Mom said at last. "I'll need to check
with your father, of course. But I suppose you can go."

"Whoo-hoo! Thanks, Mom. See you at dinner."

I hung up the phone and rushed back to the science
wing. I was hoping my name would be the first one on
the list, but there were already half a dozen names on the
page. I scrawled my name on the next empty line, eager
to hurry off to the cafeteria to find Tina and Michelle.
They didn't have science until after lunch, and I wanted
to make sure they signed up before all the spots were
filled. Mr. Truskey had explained that if more than ten
people signed up, he would try to work something out

so everyone could go. But I didn't trust that. I was in such a hurry that I didn't even bother to check out the other names on the list. I figured it didn't matter. With my two best friends along for five days and four nights of sun, sand, and environmental activism, what could go wrong?

Oh, I was so young and foolish then.

"You signed up for *what*?" Tina wrinkled her nose. That was never a good sign. Tina, Michelle, and I have been friends since our first day of first grade, and I can almost always tell what they're thinking. And I wasn't liking what I saw Tina thinking at all.

I gazed at her across the lunch table, alarmed. "Think of it as a free vacation for school credit," I said. "Come on, you guys have to sign up right away—it'll be a blast!"

Tina looked doubtful. "I don't know . . . ," she murmured, staring down at her tuna sandwich. The same kind of sandwich she brings every single day. Belatedly I remembered that Tina doesn't really like change, or surprises, or anything too new and different.

I glanced over at Michelle for help. She wasn't even paying attention as she stared across the crowded cafeteria with a gleam in her eyes. "Check it, Dani," she hissed. "Here comes your boyfriend."

Worst Class Trip Ever

My cheeks went red, and I scowled at her, wishing I'd never tried to talk to her about Josh Gallagher. Josh is on the boys' basketball team, which practices at the same time as the girls' team. I'm the only sixth grader, boy or girl, who made varsity this year, and Josh was the first one to congratulate me about it, even though he was in seventh grade and he barely knew me at the time. Ever since, he still says hi to me whenever he sees me in the halls.

Here's the thing about Josh. Most people agree that he's the cutest guy in school. I don't usually notice stuff like that—I'm not one of those annoying girls who giggles and makes a fool of herself over everything in pants. But even I couldn't help noticing Josh when I met him on the first day of school. He was standing in the lobby handing out school maps to all us new sixth graders, and something about his smile just told me right away he was cool. I made the mistake of mentioning that to my best friends, and ever since then they've been teasing me about him and calling him my boyfriend. Very funny.

"Hey, Dani," Josh said, his smile including my friends. "What's up?"

"I—buh—wee—wuh—," I stammered. At least that was how it came out. I'd fully intended to say "The sun,

the moon, and the clouds. Why do you ask?" Okay, maybe not the wittiest response ever, but way better than "I—buh—wee—wuh."

Fortunately Josh just smiled. I guess he didn't mind not getting a coherent answer. Or at least he wasn't going to show it if he did. That just shows what a nice, polite person he is.

As he moved on, Michelle smirked. "Nice going, Miss Smooth."

"Zip it," I snapped. I hate looking stupid in front of anybody, and I hate it worse than ever when the witness to my stupidity is someone cool like Josh. "Now are you guys going to sign up for this stupid island trip or not?"

When it became clear that their answer was "not," I started to panic. What had I done?

The other sixth-grade science teacher, Ms. Watson, was standing in front of the bulletin board reading the sign-up list when I rounded the corner at top speed a short while later.

"Hello, Miss McFeeney," she said when she saw me. "I see you're planning to come along on our little trip next month?"

Normally I like being called "Miss McFeeney" about as

much as I do being called by my full name. But for some reason it doesn't bother me when Ms. Watson does it. She's the head of the science department and is as calm, cool, and collected as Mr. Truskey is weird, wacky, and unpredictable. I suspected that if she hadn't been involved, taking care of the details and generally being sensible and responsible, there was probably no way Mr. Truskey could have made this trip happen.

"I—I—" For a second I was completely tongue-tied, which is totally unlike me—at least when Josh Gallagher isn't around. Finally I just shrugged. "I guess," I told her weakly. I couldn't tell her I was planning to scratch my name off the list. It just seemed way too flaky, and somehow I knew she wouldn't approve. "I came to see who else signed up," I added in a sudden burst of inspiration.

Ms. Watson smiled and nodded, then turned back toward her classroom. I took another step toward the bulletin board. Now that I'd mentioned it, I *was* sort of curious about the list. Maybe if some of my other friends went, the trip could still be sort of fun even without Michelle and Tina—

But when I got a good look at the sign-up sheet, my jaw dropped, and my eyes bugged out like some kind of

cartoon character. First on the list, written in big, fat, loopy cursive letters that just oozed snottiness, was the name ANGELA BARNES.

"Oh no," I groaned under my breath.

Ms. Watson paused in her classroom door and turned around. "What was that, Miss McFeeney?"

"Nothing. Just clearing my throat." I forced a sickly smile and turned to face the list so she wouldn't see the twitch that was developing just under my left eye. A week in the tropics with Evil Angela? That didn't sound like a vacation in paradise. It sounded like a trip to the lowest realm of Hades.

Angela Barnes is blond, prissy, snooty, and perfect—at least in her own mind. Her fingernails are always pink, her lips are always glossed, and all her clothes always match, even in gym class. I can't stand her, and the feeling is mutual. It probably all started the first week of first grade when I brought my pet frog to school, and Angela turned me in to Mrs. DiAngelo. Poor Hoppy never really recovered from those four hours inside Mrs. D's desk drawer.

That was only the beginning. I got my revenge for the Hoppy incident by putting bubble gum in Angela's hair-

brush. (Yes, she brought a hairbrush with her to class, even in first grade.) She returned the favor by starting a rumor that I'd been born a boy. I stole a pair of pink flowered underpants from her locker and hung them on the flagpole. And so on.

Eventually I guess the two of us sort of decided that life was easier if we stayed out of each other's way as much as possible. That doesn't mean we like each other any better now. It just means we're more mature than we were back in first grade. At least *I* am.

So why was she going on the trip? While I could easily imagine her signing up just to look good in front of the teachers—she's a huge teacher's pet—I couldn't begin to imagine her actually cleaning up a trash dump. She might break a nail or something. The more I thought about it, the more it irritated me, and for a second I was tempted to stick with the trip after all, if only to show Miss Priss how a real girl could help the environment.

Then I regained my sanity. I wasn't going to make myself miserable just to prove some kind of stupid point to Evil Angela.

I scanned the rest of the list. Seven of the ten spaces were already filled. The second, third, and fourth names

on the list belonged to seventh and eighth graders I knew only slightly. Ryan Rodriguez was next, followed by Cassie and her twin sister, Chrissie. Eighth, of course, was me. For the moment, at least.

I figured I'd just wait until the next day and tell Mr. Truskey I was dropping out. But when I got home from basketball practice that afternoon, I discovered that my parents had other ideas.

"Forget it, Dani," my mom said when I told her about my change of plans. "Your father and I are tired of watching you make these impulsive decisions, being all gung ho for a little while, and then changing your mind. Besides, this trip will be good for you, and . . ."

I sort of tuned out for a while then, catching an occasional word or two here and there, like "helping people," "educational," "responsibility," and "travel opportunity." And I definitely heard her last few words: "You're going, and that's final."

So that's how I found myself stuck cleaning up a smelly old trash dump on a deserted island with the craziest teacher in school, a handful of people I barely knew, *Josh Gallagher(!!!)*, the Saunders twins—and, of course, Evil Angela Barnes. For four days I sweated in the saunalike

tropical heat, I got splinters from stacking about ten tons of termite-infested wood, and I slapped mosquitoes non-stop. I also slept in a tent and shared a latrine—which I found out to my extreme horror is really just a fancy word for "big hole in the sand"—with twelve other people. During the day, we were forced to run back and forth between the baking sun on the beach and the soggy jungle of the island's interior as we dragged around metal shards and old boards. At night I did my best to sleep despite the steady whine of the mosquitoes.

Finally the searing, scorching sun rose over our last morning on the island. A short while after breakfast I emerged from the latrine's enclosure—which is just a fancy word for "a bunch of boards sort of nailed together and leaned against a tree"—and found Evil Angela tapping her perfectly pedicured toes impatiently just outside.

"About time," she snitted when she saw me.

"Sorry to interrupt your schedule, but human bodily functions take time," I replied loftily. "We can't all be cyborgs like you."

Angela just rolled her eyes and pushed past me. But another voice piped in from nearby. "Hope you didn't leave it all stinky in there like you always do at home . . . *Danielle*."

Castaways

Oh. Did I mention my obnoxious little brother, Kenny, got to come on the trip too?

"Shut up, twerp," I told him. I tell him that so often, it's sort of like breathing—it just happens without my having to think about it. Aside from our matching red hair, Kenny and I have pretty much nothing in common.

Kenny shrugged and wandered off, probably to search for more disgusting bugs and other creepy crawlies. My little brother is a typical eight-year-old—muddy, sniffly, usually a little smelly. He's always got something weird in his pockets, and he lives to embarrass me. Even though he can't seem to remember to put the toilet seat down or replace the cap on the toothpaste, he has a photographic memory for every embarrassing thing I've ever said or done. I still couldn't believe my parents had talked his way onto this trip. But somehow, giddy with the thought of having the house to themselves for the first time in eight years, they'd convinced Mr. Truskey that Kenny should come along. They even paid for his plane ticket themselves, since all the free spots were already filled. There really should be some kind of rule about parents torturing their daughters that way. It just goes to show that even when you think

things can't possibly get any worse . . . they can.

Leaving the latrine area, I headed toward the beach to see if it was time to go yet, trying to ignore Kenny trailing along after me. You know, tropical islands always look so pretty, pleasant, and peaceful on TV. Maybe there are some out there like that, but this particular island wasn't one of them. Oh, sure, it looked picturesque enough from a distance, what with the coral reef, the calm lagoon, the white sand beach, the swaying palm trees. All the stuff that you might see on a postcard. It's only when you get closer that you start to notice the other stuff—the stultifying heat, the sand that sticks to your skin and gets in your bathing suit, the mosquitoes as big as your hand.

And then there's the bug that got Robert Verden.

I guess I haven't mentioned the lesser equatorial beachwalker beetle yet. It's some obscure species of insect that looks like a cockroach on steroids, and is known to the locals as the choo-choo bug. Or maybe it's chuchu bug, I don't know. They're supposed to be incredibly rare in most places, though you'd never know it from hanging out on this particular island. There, they were everywhere—flying up in front of you when you walked, buzzing around the lanterns at night, and chomping on innocent middle schoolers every chance they got. I'm not one of those girls who are squeamish about bugs, but within hours of arrival I was pretty sick of that particular species. We'd all been bitten at least once, but it turned out that Robert was the only one on the trip allergic to the bites. When his face swelled up to twice its normal size, Ms. Watson had to take one of the two boats that brought us to the island and rush him back to civilization a day early. Lucky guy.

So now we were waiting for Ms. Watson to return with the second boat. Then it would just be an hour's seasick-making ride back to the mainland, followed by a short flight to bring us home sweet home.

Scratching the latest of the million and one mosquito bites on my arm, I wandered over to see what the twins were doing. I found them standing on the beach, arguing over whether the water in the lagoon was warmer or colder than their pool at home. I kid you not. Then again, Chrissie and Cassie argue over absolutely everything. If Chrissie says the sky is blue, Cassie will insist that it's green. If Cassie wants to play volleyball, Chrissie will declare that only kick ball will do. If Chrissie tells some-

one the twins got their dark hair and perfect cinnamon-colored skin from their African American father, Cassie will contend that they came from their Asian American mother. But even though they'd never admit it, there's lots of stuff they actually see eye to eye on. For one thing, they both agree that Angela Barnes is evil incarnate, which is why I stay friends with them even though they drive me crazy sometimes.

After a moment Josh walked by, dragging a half-rotted board behind him. Cassie's eyes widened, and she elbowed me sharply in the ribs. "Check him out," she whispered, her eyes gleaming. "How can he look so good when the rest of us are such a mess?"

Her twin giggled. "It's so cute how he doesn't even know he's so cute! Don't you think, Dani?"

I just sighed. "Whatever," I muttered, wondering when the twins had gotten so giggly and flirty and dorky. It seemed to be an epidemic—every time I turned around, another girl was turning into Angela Barnes Jr. At least Tina and Michelle and I were still normal. . . .

While I was thinking about that, Mr. Truskey came crashing out of the jungle onto the beach. Over the past four days on the island, his pasty-white skin had burned to a crispy shade of maroon, but now I noticed he was looking sort of pale again. Almost greenish. I also saw that his shirt was buttoned wrong, and he seemed to be missing one of his sandals.

"Check *him* out," I murmured to the twins, who were already arguing over whether Josh would look cuter or less cute with longer hair. "Mr. Truskey doesn't look too good."

The twins turned and watched as the teacher staggered across the beach. "No big shock," Chrissie said. "He's probably got a stomachache from eating that gross beetle last night."

Remember those choo-choo/chuchu bugs I was talking about? Well, Mr. Truskey apparently thought it must be spelled chew-chew bug. When a local tribe came over from a neighboring island for a little island-style cookout, the chief offered us all a taste of the local delicacy— grilled choo-choo bugs. The rest of us had enough sense to pretend to be full, but Mr. Truskey grabbed one of the bugs and chowed down like it was the last eggroll in a Chinese restaurant.

I rolled my eyes, realizing Chrissie was probably right. Glancing past the teacher, I saw that several of the others were trailing after him out of the jungle, including Kenny.

"People!" Mr. Truskey called, lurching toward us with his cell phone in his hand. "There you are."

"Here we are," I replied, trying not to notice that Josh was heading back toward us from the other direction, carrying his duffel bag. "So where's Ms. W? We're all packed up and ready to go."

Mr. Truskey looked sheepish. "That's what I wanted to tell you, Mary Jane," he said. "Gillian called me from the mainland a couple of hours ago. Robert is still in the hospital for observation, and she can't leave him until his parents arrive this evening. So she won't be able to make it back out here with the other boat until tomorrow morning."

I was still puzzling over the "Mary Jane" thing when the full force of what he'd said hit me. "What?" I exclaimed.

"You're kidding!" Chrissie added.

Cassie let out a shriek. "Oh no!" she wailed. "We're going to be stuck on this island for a whole extra day!"

Two

I rolled my eyes. As eager as I was to escape from the island, my first thought was that Cassie was totally overreacting to Mr. Truskey's news. Judging by the snickers from all around, everyone else agreed. Even Chrissie let out a snort.

"Take a chill pill, Sis," she said. "It's not that big a deal."

"Yes, it is," Cassie argued.

Chrissie frowned. "No, it isn't."

"Just a second," Brooke Hubbard spoke up. Brooke is the vice president of the Tweedale Student Council and the only eighth grader on the trip, which made her think

she had some kind of seniority over the rest of us. "What are you saying, Mr. Truskey?"

"Don't panic, kidaloos," Mr. Truskey replied, wiping a bead of sweat from his brow as he glanced at our one remaining boat bobbing in the surf a few yards out from the beach. "I told Gillian not to worry about us. We can all squeeze on to the other helichopper."

"You mean the other boat?" Chrissie corrected him.

"Yes, of course, that's right. Thank you, Roberta." Mr. Truskey smiled at Chrissie, who looked confused at being called by the wrong name. "The other boat. It'll be a little friendly, that's all."

I wasn't sure how "friendly" I felt like getting with Evil Angela or Annoying Kenny. Or the rest of them, for that matter—after five days without plumbing, nobody was exactly powder fresh. And the boats that had brought us to the island were barely bigger than the canoe in my grandparents' pond. Well, okay, maybe they were a little bigger than that. But my point is, they weren't exactly luxury yachts or anything.

When I felt the telltale sting of a choo-choo bug biting my ankle, I decided I didn't really care about any of that. "Okay, then," I said as brightly as I could, shaking my leg

to send the giant beetle flying. "What are we waiting for?"

"Not everybody is here yet," Brooke pointed out. "Where's Angela?"

I for one was perfectly willing to leave her behind to the choo-choo bugs and mosquitoes. But the others didn't seem to think that was a good idea. Besides, we still had to gather up our supplies and finish dismantling our camp.

Half an hour later we were all ready. I looked around at the little group gathered on the beach. Mr. Truskey was still looking kind of green around the gills, but he'd located his other sandal and seemed more with-it than before. Chrissie and Cassie were dressed in their matching shorts and T-shirts, arguing about which of them was more likely to get seasick on the trip back. Kenny was standing behind the twins, picking his nose. Ryan Rodriguez was kicking a rock around the beach as if it was a soccer ball. Brooke was bossily directing a seventh grader named Macy Walden to move her backpack out of the way so she could drag the tent poles closer to the water. Ned Campbell, a pale, pudgy sixth grader with a serious TV habit and an aversion to exercise of any kind, was staring into space, probably wondering why in the world his parents made him come on this trip and how soon he

would be back in front of Nick at Nite, where he belonged.

And Evil Angela was standing next to Josh, batting her long eyelashes at him and smiling.

I narrowed my eyes and took a step closer, wanting to hear what they were talking about. It wasn't the first time I'd noticed Angela trying to flirt with Josh, and I didn't like it one bit. Even if I wasn't really interested in him *that way* myself—no matter what Michelle and Tina might think—I definitely didn't want the Evil One to get him. He deserved better than that. Way better.

"Ready, everyone?" Mr. Truskey called out. "Time to get back on the bus and get out of here."

"The boat, Mr. Truskey," Brooke corrected helpfully.

Mr. Truskey blinked at her. "What's that, Lillian?"

"It's Brooke," Brooke said. "And I said it's a boat."

I exchanged a worried glance with the twins. Mr. Truskey might be on the wacky side, but he usually doesn't have any trouble remembering his students' names—or the names of common forms of transportation, either.

"Of course it's a boat!" Mr. Truskey smiled brightly. "How else are we supposed to get off this island? Now let's go!"

We all waded out through the gentle surf toward the

boat. As I pulled myself aboard, I glanced back at the island. A slight breeze made the palms seem to dance, and the sunlight sparkling off the gentle waves turned the lagoon into a field of diamonds. The whole scene looked so peaceful and beautiful that for a split second I almost wished we didn't have to leave.

Then I came to my senses. "Anchors away!" I cried, already counting the seconds until I was back in the land of showers, real toilets, and non-bug-related food.

Angela rolled her eyes. "Dork," she muttered, just loud enough for me to hear.

I merely smiled sweetly in response. Not even Evil Angela could bother me when home was so close I could taste it. Besides, I knew it would bug her like crazy if she thought her snotty comments didn't bother me at all.

Half an hour later I was sitting on the bench in the back of the boat, watching the churned-up water of our wake recede behind us and chatting with Macy Walden. Macy is one of those kids who is weird enough that she should stand out, but instead she just sort of blends into the background, like a ripped spot in the wallpaper that you don't notice after a while. She wears these frilly, lacey,

flowery clothes that look handmade and sort of old-fashioned, and I doubt her long, straight brown hair has ever seen a drop of conditioner.

"And so I wasn't going to come after all, but then my parents said I had no choice," I was saying in response to Macy's question about why I'd come on the island trip. "So at that point I decided I might as well make the best of it and try to have fun if possible. Especially since it was such a good cause and everything." I shrugged. "But enough about me. What made you decide to come?"

Macy fiddled with the delicate silver bracelet she was wearing. "I've always been interested in environmental issues," she said, her soft voice barely audible above the steady chug-chug-chug of the boat's motor. "I guess it's because of my older brother. He's an environmental lobbyist up in Washington."

"Really? Cool. I didn't know that."

Actually, I didn't know much of anything about Macy. I don't think we'd said more than three words to each other before the start of the trip, partly because she was in seventh grade and I was in sixth, but mostly because she tended to keep to herself at school. I'm pretty outgoing, but I don't usually bother trying to

befriend the geeks and weirdoes who lurk around the fringes of middle-school society. Someone as popular as Josh can get away with that sort of thing—he's friendly to everybody—but I never figured it was worth risking my own popularity.

Until now. The trip back to the mainland seemed to be taking forever, the twins were busy arguing about something stupid, and I was desperate for any kind of company that didn't involve my grubby little brother.

"Hey, Dani," Kenny called, hurrying toward us as if reading my mind. He skidded on a wet patch on the floor, almost flying off over the back of the boat. He caught himself just in time.

"What is it, dork boy?" I asked.

Kenny reached into his pocket. "Look," he said with a grin.

He held out his hand. Two choo-choo bugs were nestled there, their pincers opening and closing irritably.

I shuddered. "Get those things away from me!" I snapped.

Macy was leaning closer. "Be careful, Kenny," she said. "Remember, those guys are an endangered species. You probably shouldn't keep them as pets. They're too important."

"Really?" Kenny's eyes widened. "I didn't know that." He stared down at the huge bugs. "Maybe I'll give them to Ms. Gillian when we get back."

I wrinkled my nose. It irritated me that Kenny was allowed to call Ms. Watson by her first name when the rest of us weren't. Then again, most things about Kenny irritated me.

"Get lost, twerp," I snarled. "And take those stinkbugs with you."

Kenny smirked at me as he tucked the bugs back in his pocket. "You're just in a bad mood because Angela's prettier than you," he taunted. "That's probably why she's hogging your *boyfriend*, Josh."

He danced off before I could react. Feeling my cheeks burn red, I glanced around wildly, hoping that nobody else had heard. Luckily the twins were the only other people in the back part of the boat except for Ned, who was sitting in the shade of the cabin overhang, listening to his portable radio with the headphones. The rest of the kids were up in front, sunbathing or playing cards, while Mr. Truskey was down in the cabin steering.

I smiled weakly at Macy. "Kenny doesn't know what he's talking about. He's just being a jerk."

"Sure." She smiled, ducking her head and looking almost as embarrassed as I felt. "It's no big deal. He's just a kid."

I sighed loudly. "Boy, will I be glad to get back to civilization."

"Me too," Macy agreed. "But look on the bright side. At least we did some good on this trip. We cleaned up that island and made it more habitable for the wildlife that lives there."

"I guess." I was having trouble looking on the bright side at the moment. Sure, the wildlife might be a little happier, but all I had to show for it were bug bites and blisters. As I glanced over at the island we were passing at the moment, though, I had to admit it was awfully pretty. "Check out the huge waterfall," I said. "I didn't notice that on the way—"

The boat lurched violently, interrupting me in mid-sentence. I was flung to one side, crashing into Macy. Both of us tumbled to the floor. Nearby, the twins shrieked as they were thrown off their feet.

"Whoa!" Ryan shouted from somewhere out of sight beyond the cabin. "What's happening?"

I pushed myself to a sitting position and grabbed the edge of the bench just in time as the boat pitched to the

other side. "Yikes," I said. "What was that all about?"

The water was calm all around us, and the air barely qualified as breezy. What had made the boat rock like that?

"Come on!" Brooke was hurrying around from the front deck, followed by the others. "We'd better check on Mr. Truskey."

I was the first one to follow her down into the cabin. As soon as I peered inside, Brooke and I both gasped.

"Mr. T!" I cried.

The teacher was slumped over the wheel. He was sort of tilted to one side, which I guess explained the sudden lurching.

The others all crowded into the doorway behind us. "What's happening?" Ryan yelled again.

"Oh no!" Angela squealed. "Mr. Truskey's in trouble!" She pushed her way forward, shoving me into the wall as she passed. "Let me through—I'm qualified in first aid."

I snorted. I wasn't about to let her take over and try to make herself look good, as usual. "Yeah, right," I said. "Reading about first aid on the back of your Cheerios box doesn't make you qualified."

When I leaned over Mr. Truskey, I saw that his eyes

were half-open. He wasn't actually unconscious or any-thing—just limp and sort of woozy-looking.

"Move it," Angela muttered at me, trying to push me aside as she leaned over him too.

"There you are, Mary Ann," Mr. Truskey mumbled, his eyes fluttering as he focused on me. "You know, my stomach doesn't feel quite right. I believe that beach-walker beetle may have been a bad—"

"Uh-oh." I stepped back as a shudder ran through the teacher's entire body. "Looks like he's going to—"

Spla-a-at!

Without further warning, Mr. Truskey emptied what seemed to be the entire contents of his stomach all over the cabin. Angela and I both jumped back just in time to avoid most of the flying barf. A few specks landed on my sneakers. I frantically tried to rub them off on the wall, glad I hadn't worn my flip-flops that morning.

"Gross!" Chrissie and Cassie shrieked loudly in unison, in a rare moment of perfect agreement. There was a lot of screaming and shouting as everyone suddenly decided the cabin wasn't the place to be after all. Well, except for Kenny. Now that vomit was involved, he was more interested than ever.

"Let me see!" he shouted, pushing his way past Josh and jumping forward toward the wheel.

"Move it, loser boy." I shoved him aside, sending him skidding through a puddle of puke. He caught himself just in time by grabbing the wheel, causing the boat to jerk sideways again. Mr. Truskey lost his weak grip on the wheel. I winced as his head struck the floor with a solid *thunk*.

"Ohhhh, I'm going to hurl!" Chrissie moaned from the doorway, holding her nose. "This is too disgusting!"

Suddenly Macy pushed past the twins. "Hey!" Cassie protested.

Macy ignored her. She stepped forward and grabbed the wheel with both hands, not even seeming to notice the slimy vomit dripping from it.

"What are you doing?" Brooke snapped at her, sounding annoyed and a little panicky. I guess this sort of thing didn't happen very often at student-council meetings.

Macy took one hand off the wheel just long enough to point out the window straight ahead. My eyes widened as I noticed for the first time that the boat, which was still chugging along at top speed, was about twenty yards from plowing straight into the tall, jagged edge of a huge coral reef!

Three

"Look out!" Brooke screeched uselessly.

I felt frozen into place. Some vague, distant part of my brain was blinking an alert, trying to convince me to take some sort of action, but the rest of me was completely ignoring the call. All I could do was stand there and wait for my life to flash before my eyes, or whatever it is that's supposed to happen in your last moments.

Meanwhile Macy was spinning the wheel to the left, hauling on it with more strength than I would've thought she had in her thin, gingham-dressed body. The boat seemed to groan in protest, its wooden frame mak-

ing all sorts of ominous creaking sounds. But slowly, slowly . . . it turned. There were a few bumps and thumps from somewhere near the hull, but we skidded past the bulk of the coral with just a couple of feet to spare.

As the boat cleared the reef and chugged back out toward the open channel between islands, there was a moment of silence. I think we were all in shock at the close call.

"Whew!" Josh said at last. "Nice going, Macy. Thanks."

"Yeah, three cheers for Macy!" Ryan shouted, pumping his fist in the air.

Kenny clapped his hands. "Hip, hip hooray!"

Everyone else started babbling their own thanks. Even Angela, who had probably never spoken to Macy before in her life, shot the other girl a fake-looking smile and mumbled something complimentary.

"Okay, that's fine, but we still have a problem here." Brooke sounded slightly sour as she gestured toward Mr. Truskey. I guess she didn't like seeing someone else getting all that praise.

Still, she had a point. Mr. Truskey's chest was rising and falling steadily as he lay there on the floor, but his breathing sounded a little burbly. That couldn't be good.

"Should we move him outside or something?" I suggested. "Maybe some fresh air would help him feel better."

"I guess." Brooke sounded dubious, but nobody seemed to have any other ideas. "Come on, then. Macy, you stay here and steer the boat while the rest of us take care of this."

"What?" Macy sounded nervous. "Um, I don't really know what I'm doing here. Besides, which way are we supposed to—"

"Just steer, all right?" Brooke snapped. She glanced around at the rest of us. "Dani, Angela, Ned, and Ryan—you guys grab his arms. Josh, Cassie, and Chrissie can take his legs."

"What are *you* going to do?" Chrissie asked, not looking at all thrilled about the idea of touching the teacher's bare, hairy, vomit-spattered legs. I couldn't blame her. His arms didn't look much better.

"I'll direct you, so you don't bump him into anything," Brooke replied in an I'm-the-kindergarten-teacher-so-don't-question-me sort of voice.

It took a few minutes and a little more arguing, but we managed to gingerly lift, push, haul, and drag Mr. Truskey up the four or five steps from the cabin and onto the rear deck. He still seemed to be half-conscious at

best, occasionally moaning something about bugs and tribal customs. Kenny tagged along, offering helpful comments such as "Don't drop him" and "Watch out for that barf puddle. Oops, too late."

"I have an idea," Ryan said eagerly, once Mr. Truskey was sprawled out on the deck. Without waiting for a response, he raced off to the side of the boat. Grabbing the bucket that was lashed there, he leaned over the edge.

I gasped. "Careful!" I cried as I saw him start to lose his balance. Jumping toward him, I grabbed him around the waist and hauled him back into the boat.

He landed on his rear end with a thump, spilling about a third of his bucket all over my sneakers. "Thanks, Dani," he said with a grin.

"What the heck are you doing, Ryan?" Brooke demanded. "We have enough problems without you falling overboard or something."

Ignoring her, Ryan clambered to his feet and grabbed his bucket. Skidding across the wet deck toward Mr. Truskey, he dumped the water straight over the teacher's face.

Mr. Truskey sputtered and sat up, his eyes flying wide open. "Go west, young man!" he shouted at the top of his lungs.

Then he slumped back onto the deck. His eyes drifted shut, and a second later he started snoring loudly.

I stared down at him. "Well, at least that cleaned off some of the vomit," I offered weakly, trying to look for that bright side Macy was talking about earlier.

Brooke rolled her eyes. "Yeah, real helpful," she said sarcastically. "Listen, people. We can't just act crazy here. If you have an idea, you need to discuss it with the group before you just go ahead and do it, all right?" She glared at Ryan.

Meanwhile Josh kneeled down next to Mr. Truskey. "He's out like a light," he commented. "Do you guys think that 'Go west' comment meant anything?"

"I don't know," Angela said. "What do *you* think, Josh?"

Josh shrugged. "Not sure. And maybe it doesn't matter. How are we supposed to know which way is west?" He squinted up at the sun, which was more or less directly overhead by that point.

"I know."

Everyone turned to stare at Ned. He was standing in the shade of the cabin stairwell, his radio clutched in one plump hand.

"Huh?" Brooke said.

Ned shrugged, looking bashful. "I said I know how to tell which way is west," he said. "You just need to blah-blah-blah sun blah-blah."

That's not really what he said, of course. It was some kind of mumbo jumbo about angles and reflections and the horizon and who knows what else.

I glanced around. Most of the others looked as skeptical as I felt. Like I said, Ned isn't exactly Mr. Outdoorsy. Personally I was a little surprised that he knew there *was* a sun.

"How do you know all that?" Angela demanded.

"I saw it on TV," Ned responded calmly. "See, you just have to figure out blah-blah-blah . . ."

I tuned out on the specifics, and I guess everyone else did too. Only Kenny was nodding along eagerly. "Cool!" he said when Ned finished. "That's awesome!"

"Okay, whatever." Brooke was already heading for the cabin. "Let's go see if there's a compass or something inside. Maybe even some kind of two-way radio."

The rest of us drifted after her. The twins fell into step on either side of me. "Do you guys think 'Go west' actually means anything?" I asked them. "I mean, Truskey isn't scoring too high on the Coherent Meter right now."

"Good point." Cassie looked worried. "It probably doesn't mean anything at all."

Her twin shrugged. "We don't know that," she said. "And it's not like we have any better plan...."

They continued arguing about it, but I stopped listening. I was watching as Angela pretended to trip on the top step leading down to the cabin. She grabbed onto Josh's arm to steady herself, and continued clinging to it as they disappeared into the cabin behind Brooke. Nearby, Kenny was watching them too. He turned to stare at me with a big grin on his grubby little face.

I gritted my teeth. It was way past time to get off this boat—we needed to get back to the mainland before I threw a couple of people overboard.

Hurrying into the cabin, I wrinkled my nose as the unmistakable aroma of fresh barf hit me. Brooke didn't even seem to notice the stench as she stood with her hands on her hips, arguing with Macy, while Josh looked on with concern. "What's going on?" I asked.

Macy glanced at me, her big hazel eyes worried. "Dani, don't you think maybe we should just drop anchor and stay put?" she said. "It seems like that would make it a lot easier for someone to find us if Mr. Truskey doesn't

recover soon. Especially since we don't even know which way to go."

"But we *do* know which way to go," Brooke said impatiently. "I just *told* you. All we have to do is figure out which way is west."

"Well . . . ," Josh began, sounding doubtful.

"Forget it," I blurted out. "Sitting around won't do us any good. We might as well keep moving."

Macy looked slightly hurt, but I did my best to ignore it. There was no way I wanted to just sit there at the end of an anchor, like a toy boat bobbing in a bathtub, waiting for who-knows-how-long until Mr. Truskey woke up or someone noticed we were missing.

Everyone except Macy agreed. Nobody wanted to stay on that small, creaky, stinky boat a second longer than necessary. Brooke took over the steering, with Ned standing by trying to convince her she was going the wrong way. I still had my doubts about the "Go west" directions to begin with, but I figured it didn't matter. Any direction was better than no direction at all.

"Maybe you should give Ned a shot," I suggested after a while. "He might know what he's talking about."

Josh opened his mouth. I held my breath, certain that

he was going to agree with me about Ned.

But before he could speak, Angela snorted. "Get real, Dani."

Ned looked hurt. "I keep telling you, I—"

"Quiet!" Brooke snapped. "I'm trying to get us home here, okay?"

"How can you do that if you don't know which way you're going?" Chrissie put in tentatively.

Angela scowled at her. "Hey, at least Brooke is willing to try," she said. "I think we should support her."

I rolled my eyes. That was typical Angela—you could always count on her to stick up for the overdog. "Whatever," I muttered. "I'm just saying, maybe Ned could be right. Stranger things have happened."

We all argued about it for a few more minutes. Brooke kept busy steering around the islands, which seemed to be scattered in this part of the sea as thickly as dandelions in an unmowed lawn.

"Hey," she interrupted after a while. "Did anyone look around for a radio like I suggested? Most ships have those, right?"

"I wouldn't exactly call this a ship," I muttered. But I glanced around the cabin. "Oh. Is that the radio there?"

Josh leaped toward the two-way radio receiver hanging on the wall near the door. "Good eye, Dani!" he said. He fiddled with the radio for a second, looking hopeful, but then his face fell. "I can't get a signal."

"Let me try," Kenny said eagerly. He grabbed the radio out of Josh's hand and examined it. "Whoa. I think it's busted."

I rolled my eyes. "Thanks, oh Expert One," I said sarcastically.

"No, he's right," Josh said sadly. "It's totally busted. Looks like it hasn't worked in years."

"Look, you guys." Ned's voice was getting a little whiny. "You can see which way the sun's moving now—toward the *west*. We should be going *that* way, just like I said before."

Glancing up, I saw that he was right. How much time had passed since Mr. Truskey's barf-o-rama? I wasn't sure, but the sun had definitely shifted in the meantime.

We all squinted up through the window for a moment. "I think he's right," Josh said. "Sorry for not trusting you, dude." He smiled apologetically at Ned, then glanced around at the rest of us. "What do you say? Should we switch directions?"

"I vote yes," Angela said immediately.

"Me too," I added, glaring at her. Why did she always have to be such a suck-up? Not that Josh wasn't probably right, but she didn't have to be so Happy-Miss-Pep-Rally about it.

"Do whatever you want." Brooke abruptly released the wheel. "I'm going up on deck to check on Mr. Truskey. If he's awake, I'll see if he has his cell phone on him so we can call the mainland."

Josh grabbed the wheel as she hurried out of the cabin. "Okay, Ned," he said. "Which way?"

Ned pointed off to the left. Josh swung the wheel that way, though he had to steer right again within a few minutes when another small island loomed up ahead. "Lots of little islands in this part of the chain," he muttered.

We were all silent for a few minutes, staring out the window. I peered toward the horizon ahead, waiting for a glimpse of the mainland. But all that appeared were more islands, some of them larger than the one we'd just left and others smaller than my backyard at home.

"Hey," Ryan spoke up after a while, staring out at a weird-looking coral outcropping. "Was anyone paying attention to the scenery on our trip out here the other day? Because the stuff we're passing isn't looking too familiar."

I bit my lip, realizing I'd been thinking the same thing for at least the past twenty minutes or so. I just hadn't wanted to admit it, even to myself.

"I think he's right," Chrissie said. "We're totally going the wrong way."

Cassie shook her head. "We don't know that. There are a million islands out here, and they all look alike. I remember telling Mr. T that on our way out here."

Josh clutched the wheel tightly as he steered past the coral. "I don't know," he said, sounding worried. "I can't say I memorized what we saw on the way out or anything. But it seems like if we're going the right way, things should be starting to look familiar by now, right?"

I was starting to have a very bad feeling about this. I glanced at Macy, who wasn't saying anything. "Maybe you were right in the first place," I told her. "We probably should've stayed put after Mr. Truskey conked out."

Macy smiled gratefully, but Angela glared at me. "Come on, Dani," she snapped. "It's too late for that now. If you must speak—and I know you must—why don't you at least try to be helpful?"

"Fine," I snapped back. I was ready to say a few more choice words, but I didn't want to get into a fight with

her in front of the others. Instead I turned and stomped toward the steps. "I'm going to see if I can *help* Brooke figure out a way to *help* Mr. Truskey wake up, so he can *help* us get home, all right?"

Without waiting for an answer, I hurried up onto the deck. Brooke was crouched over Mr. Truskey, waving one hand in front of his face. Her other hand was on her knee. She's African American with pretty dark skin, but I could see that the knuckles on that hand had gone a little paler than the rest of her, which meant she had to be clenching pretty hard. She glanced up at me.

"He's out like a light," she said, her voice shaking slightly. "I think he's okay—he's breathing and snoring and everything—but I can't wake him up. And I don't see his cell phone anywhere."

I kneeled down on the other side of Mr. Truskey's limp figure. "Did you check his pockets?"

Brooke shuddered slightly. "Um, well, it's not in his shirt pocket," she said. "His shorts are all full of vomit."

At that moment the teacher let out a loud snort and shifted positions, rolling over onto his side and snuggling up to the wooden deck like it was a down pillow. My eyes widened. A small canvas holster was strapped to

his belt, and sticking out of it was a cell phone.

"There it is!" I cried.

Brooke reached for it gingerly, using two fingers as she tried to avoid the spatters of dried vomit. "Oh, ick," she murmured.

Her fingers brushed against the hem of Mr. Truskey's shirt, shifting the fabric. He started, giggling slightly in his sleep.

"Don't tickle him," I said.

"I can't help it," Brooke complained. "If you think you can do better . . ."

As she glanced up at me irritably, her hand dropped and poked him in the side again. This time Mr. Truskey laughed out loud and sat straight up, almost conking Brooke's head with his own.

"Stop, stop, I give!" he shouted with another laugh, his eyes flying open. "Just stop the tickling, Samantha!" He blinked and looked around at us groggily. "Oh. Girls. What are you two doing in this igloo?"

"We were just going to borrow your phone, Mr. T." Brooke gestured at the cell phone, which was sticking halfway out of its holster.

The others must have heard the commotion. The twins,

Ryan, Angela, and Kenny appeared in the cabin doorway.

Chrissie stepped forward. "We seem to be a little off course," she told the teacher. "We should probably call the mainland for help."

Mr. Truskey nodded slowly. "Good answer, young lady," he said, his words slightly slurred so they sounded like "Goo ashwu, yuh layuh." He grabbed the phone from his belt. "Here you go—catch!"

With that, he winged the phone in what he probably thought was Chrissie's general direction. Unfortunately his aim was way off. The phone flew up in a graceful arc—up, up, and away, right over the rail of the boat. In the stunned silence we all heard the tiny *splash!* as it hit the water.

"We've got to get it back!" Ryan shouted, diving for the edge of the boat.

"No!" Brooke yelped, grabbing his arm just in time to stop him from leaping overboard. "Wait!"

"Let him go!" Cassie shrieked. "We need that phone!"

Angela shook her head. "Shut up, spaz," she ordered Cassie. "Think about it. We're in enough trouble as it is without someone jumping off the boat and getting eaten by sharks or something."

"Yeah, right," I said. "Sharks. *That's* exactly what we should be worrying about right now."

"Maybe we could find a fishing net or something," Chrissie suggested. "Fish the phone out that way."

"I didn't see any fishing nets," Cassie replied anxiously, tears welling up in her dark eyes.

"Quiet!" Brooke shouted, clapping her hands for attention. "We need to think about this. There are life vests in the storage hold. Is it worth letting someone put one on and trying to get the phone?"

Kenny shrugged. "Uh-uh," he responded calmly. "Not worth it. That phone was ruined the second it hit the salt water."

Brooke glared at him for a second. It was obvious that Kenny wasn't the one she'd been expecting to respond to her question.

But it was also obvious to all of us that he was right. I couldn't help being momentarily impressed. His surprisingly logical and smart comment might have just saved us a lot of wasted effort.

Still, even a stopped clock is right twice a day. Besides, I had more important things to worry about than whether Kenny the Kreep was actually growing a brain.

Castaways

"The dork is right," I said to the others. "Forget the phone. Time for Plan B."

Mr. Truskey's eyes had glazed over again. He started groggily singing some kind of sea shanty, obviously unaware of what had just happened. Leaving him to it, we all wandered back into the cabin and told Josh, Macy, and Ned the news.

"Great," Josh muttered grimly, gripping the wheel a little harder. I'd never seen him look so anxious. "Just great. There's still no sign of the mainland up ahead. It should definitely be visible by now if we're going the right way. Plus, none of the islands we're passing look familiar at all."

Ned nodded. "And we haven't seen any smoke for a long time," he added. "The larger islands closest to the mainland were almost all populated, remember? We should be seeing signs of that by now."

I glanced out the window toward the nearest island, where a broad, pristine white sand beach ended abruptly in a lush tangle of jungle that climbed a steep wave to the bare, rocky peak at the center of the island. Craggy cliffs rose up at one end of the beach, and a peaceful, aqua blue lagoon was ringed with a jagged shelf of coral reef. There

were no puffs of smoke, buildings, or any other sign that humans had ever set foot on the place, and my heart sank as I realized Ned and Josh were right.

"We've probably been going the wrong way this whole time," I said. "Maybe we should drop anchor now, before we get even more lost."

"Don't be stupid, Dani," Angela spoke up quickly. "I'm sure if we keep going, Josh can find our way home."

Josh shook his head, quickly stepping back from the wheel. "No way," he said. "It's someone else's turn to steer. I'm done."

Nobody seemed eager to step forward. Finally Angela reached for the wheel. "All right, Josh," she said, as if he'd offered her a personal invitation. "I guess I can take over for a while if you want."

I wasn't about to let that happen. With Angela at the helm, we'd probably end up in Timbuktu. "Forget it," I said, grabbing the wheel myself. "I'll do it."

"Quit it, *Daniel!*" Angela whined, shoving at me with her shoulder. "I said I'll do it, okay?"

"Not okay," I replied through gritted teeth, doing my best to push her away without loosening my own grip on the wheel.

Castaways

"Knock it off, both of you!" Brooke commanded irritably. "I think we should take a vote on what to do."

"But someone has to—ow!" I cried as Angela slammed her shoulder into mine again. She was a lot bonier than she looked.

"Let me up there!" Kenny shouted, leaping forward gleefully. "I'll help!"

The last thing we needed was my troublemaking little brother getting involved and making a bad situation even worse. "Out of the way, twerp," I snapped, letting go of the wheel with one hand just long enough to block his grab for it.

"Oof!" Kenny stumbled back, bumping into Brooke, who was stepping toward us with an annoyed look on her face.

"Look out!" Cassie shrieked as Brooke and Kenny staggered forward, trying to stay on their feet. A second later they crashed into Angela, sending her right into the wheel.

"Let go, Angela!" Ned cried. "You're making the boat sway!"

"Tell *her* to let go!" Angela exclaimed.

There was a moment of chaos. I tried to ram Angela out of the way so I could get the boat back under con-

trol. Angela tried to hold on, probably just to spite me. Kenny grabbed at the wheel again, while Ryan, Brooke, and Chrissie also jumped forward, arguing about who should steer. There was a brief struggle, with everyone shouting at once so it was impossible to hear anything. The boat careened wildly, spinning in circles as people yanked the wheel this way and that.

Suddenly there was a loud, shrill scream. I just had time to glance over my shoulder and see Cassie's terrified face staring out the window.

Krrrrrunch!

The boat stopped short with a sickening thud.

Four

It took a few seconds to figure out
what had just happened. Rubbing the bumps on my
shoulder, hip, and head, I staggered to my feet, leaning
on the wheel and staring out the window. "It's a reef," I
said blankly. "We hit it."

About a hundred yards ahead of us, across the lagoon,
I could see the pristine white beach I'd been looking at
moments ago. Much closer were lots of pinkish, rocky,
sharp-looking bits of coral.

"Well, duh," Angela said sourly, brushing some dust off
her pink denim shorts. "That's what you get for trying to
grab the wheel like that."

I opened my mouth to respond, but Brooke beat me to it. "Never mind," she said. "It wasn't Dani's fault; it wasn't really anyone's fault. None of us was paying enough attention, and now we've got to deal with it."

Angela gave the older girl a simpering smile. "I guess you're right, Brooke," she said. "Sorry."

I rolled my eyes, noticing she didn't apologize to me. Typical.

In the meantime Josh hurried out of the cabin, returning a moment later with a grim expression on his face. "It's pretty bad," he reported. "The coral's really sharp. The reef took out, like, one whole side of the hull. The boat will probably sink at the next high tide."

"That's only about four hours away," Ned put in helpfully.

This time nobody bothered to ask how he knew that. We just stared at one another in shock.

"So what do we do?" Ryan asked at last.

The question seemed to shake Brooke out of her stupor. "We get ourselves off this boat and onto that island," she said briskly, pointing toward the beach on the other side of the lagoon. "And we only have four hours to do it, so we'd better get moving."

"You're totally right, Brooke," Angela said in her best

sucking-up voice. "What should we do first?"

And just like that, Brooke somehow became our leader.

"Dani, you and the twins start gathering everything we might be able to use, like food and flashlights and stuff," she ordered as confidently as if she were assigning seats at a student-council meeting. "Ned, you grab everybody's luggage from the hold. Macy can help you. We'll pile everything up there for now." She pointed to the right side of the front deck, which was the closest part of the boat to the island. "Josh, Ryan," she went on, "see if you can rig up some sort of raft to carry the stuff across. Otherwise we'll just have to leave whatever isn't waterproof."

"What about me?" Kenny spoke up.

Brooke blinked at him. I think she'd forgotten he was there. Not that I could blame her—I often try to do the same thing myself.

"Oh," she said. "Um, we'll want to get out the life vests. They're in the storage hold, I think—just bring them up and put them with the rest of the stuff for now."

The rest of us just sort of shrugged and went along with Brooke's orders. However, as the twins and I were lugging a bunch of canned food up the cabin steps about fifteen minutes later, I couldn't help noticing that all

Angela was doing was standing near the growing pile of luggage, life vests, and other supplies, holding a tablet of paper and a pencil.

"Have you noticed that Angela seems to be getting all the easy jobs?" I commented breathlessly, wiping the sweat off my face. It was midafternoon by now, and the way the tropical sun was beating down made me feel like an egg sizzling on some giant boat-shaped grill. The twins and I were on about our fifth trip up from belowdecks. We had started with the easy stuff, like plastic flatware, napkins, and matches, but now all that was left was the heavier stuff like cans and bottles.

Chrissie rolled her eyes. "Figures," she said. "She's been sucking up to Brooke since the crash. Guess it paid off."

Just then Angela glanced over and spotted us. "Hurry up, girls," she called. "The sooner you get that stuff over here, the sooner I can add it to the list."

"The sooner I get up there, the sooner I can wing this can of creamed corn at her head," I muttered under my breath. Chrissie and Cassie giggled, which made me feel slightly better. At least I wasn't the only one who saw through Angela's antics.

Just then Brooke strode around the cabin and spotted

us struggling along. "Hurry up!" she said sharply. "I was just in the galley, and there's tons more food to bring up."

"If you were just in the galley, why didn't you carry some food up yourself?" Chrissie muttered breathlessly, grabbing at a can of tomato paste that was slipping out of her arms. She missed, and the can bounced to the deck.

If Brooke heard her, she pretended not to. She picked up the can and then glanced at her watch. "I want all the kitchen stuff out here in the next ten minutes, okay?" she said. "I think Ned and Macy are almost finished bringing up the luggage—they can help you. Oh, and don't forget to check the bathroom for toilet paper and stuff."

Cassie wrinkled her nose. "We already brought up like two whole six-packs of TP," she pointed out. "How much do you think we're really going to need?"

"Don't argue, okay?" Brooke replied, sounding edgy. "Just hurry up, or the boat will sink before we can get everything off. We don't need another disaster like that."

If there's one thing I can't stand, it's someone who bosses people around and exaggerates her own importance. "Get real, Brooke," I said. "It's not like we're leaving for six months in outer space. I don't see why you're making us lug around all these heavy cans of food and stuff."

Worst Class Trip Ever

"Think about it, Dani," Brooke frowned at me. "Nobody knows where we are, and we don't have cell phones or any other way of contacting the mainland. It could be hours before they find us—maybe even overnight!"

Macy had just appeared on deck with two backpacks slung over her shoulders and a large, overstuffed duffel bag in her arms. "It might be even longer than that," she put in softly.

"Brooke!" Angela called, interrupting before anyone could respond to Macy's comment. "Come check out Josh's raft. It's awesome!"

Turning, I saw Josh and Ryan dragging a makeshift concoction of wood and rope around the other side of the cabin. The base was made out of a large piece of wood. Spotting a knob still sticking out on one side, I recognized the door to the boat's small, foul-smelling bathroom. The guys had lashed a few empty plastic bottles to the bottom edges of the door/raft, along with a bunch of other bits of wood that I guessed were supposed to make the whole thing float better.

"*Cuidado, hermano,*" Josh murmured as Ryan moved forward a little too quickly, almost banging the raft into the cabin wall. "Take it easy."

"*Sí*," Ryan responded with a grin, slowing down immediately. "*Lo siento.*"

Josh and Ryan both speak fluent Spanish—Josh's mom is Cuban, while Ryan's whole family just moved to Florida a couple of years ago from Puerto Rico. It looked like the two guys had bonded over that while building their raft. That just proved once again that Josh could get along with everyone, from an obnoxious flirt like Angela to a hyperactive spazmoid like Ryan.

We all hurried over to take a closer look. Brooke seemed pleased as she nudged at the raft with the toe of her sneaker. "Looks good, guys," she told Josh and Ryan.

"We realized the door was light and sturdy and pretty big," Ryan began eagerly. "Then we thought about what other kinds of stuff would float the best, and—"

"Fine, whatever." Brooke waved him off in midexplanation. "Let's just see if it will float."

Josh and Ryan carefully lowered their creation into the water lapping up against the coral-mutilated side of the boat. I held my breath and crossed my fingers. The raft bobbed up and down a few times in the current, but it stayed afloat.

"Wahoo!" Kenny cheered.

Everyone laughed, then added cheers of their own.

"Okay, people," Brooke said, sounding relieved. "Everyone go grab one last load from the galley, and then I think we're good to go."

This time even Brooke and Angela joined in as we all hurried belowdecks to clear out the cabinets and shelves in the boat's small kitchen area and pantry. I still had my doubts about lugging all that stuff over to the island, but it didn't seem worth arguing the point.

With Brooke calling out directions, we all started fastening things to the raft using the rest of the rope the boys had found. Soon it was piled high with food, luggage, and other supplies. By then it was riding a little lower in the water, but it still appeared seaworthy.

"Okay." Brooke rubbed her hands together. "First, let's agree on a plan for the next step." Apparently in Brookese, "agreeing to a plan" is some kind of shorthand for "listening to my plan and agreeing that it's brilliant and perfect." Because she didn't even pause for a breath before going on. "The most important thing is getting the raft over to the beach in one piece."

I wasn't so sure about that. In my opinion the most important thing was getting *myself* to the beach in one

piece. But I kept my mouth shut as Brooke continued.

"That means the strongest people should be the ones who swim alongside the raft and push it along," she said. She glanced around at us. "Josh, Ryan, Ned, and, um, Dani. You guys can do that."

Angela smirked at me. "That's right," she said. "Might as well stick *Daniel* in there with the rest of the boys."

Before I could concoct a worthy comeback, Ned raised his hand. I guess Brooke was acting so much like a teacher that he thought he was back in school. "Excuse me," he said calmly. "I'm not sure that's such a good idea. See, I can't swim."

We all turned to stare at him. Brooke's eyes looked about ready to bug out of her head. "What?" she said, clearly hoping against hope that she'd misheard him.

"I said, I can't swim," Ned repeated.

I guess it shouldn't have been any huge shock. Ned is probably the laziest kid in the whole sixth grade. He doesn't play any sports, never even bothered to learn how to ride a bike, and probably considers changing the channel with the TV remote to be strenuous exercise. Why would anyone assume he knew how to swim?

A moment of hubbub followed. Brooke just continued

staring at Ned, stunned by the unexpected hole in her own brilliant plan.

Finally Josh spoke up above the ruckus. "Don't worry, guys. I think there's more wood we can use down below," he said. "It won't take long to mock up another raft out of the storage-room door. Ned can ride on that, and a couple of us can push him."

"What if I fall off?" Ned sounded nervous.

Brooke shrugged. "That's what these are for." Striding over to the pile of life vests, she grabbed one and tossed it to him. "While we're at it, everyone else had better grab a vest and strap it on."

"Why?" Ryan said. "The rest of us all know how to swim, right?"

I sneaked a peek at Kenny, remembering that my little brother had just started swimming lessons the previous June. He'd already moved up a couple of levels by the end of the summer, but he definitely wasn't ready for the Olympics yet or anything. He was staring at his feet, probably dreaming up new ways to torture me. I shrugged and returned my attention to the others.

"Just do it," Brooke was telling Ryan impatiently. "Even if you can swim pretty well, you never know if there are dangerous currents or something out there. Better safe than sorry."

We all dove for the pile of vests. When I looked around again after fastening mine around my chest, everyone had one on except for Josh and Kenny.

"I didn't get one," Kenny said, his lower lip trembling. He glanced at me. "Dani? I didn't get a vest."

"It's okay, Kenny." Macy was already unstrapping her vest. "You can have mine. I think I can swim well enough to go without."

"Thanks." Kenny smiled up at her, looking all dewy-eyed and innocent. I just rolled my eyes, glad I hadn't fallen for his boo-hoo-poor-little-me act. That kid could talk a starving man out of the last chocolate-chip cookie on Earth.

Brooke glanced at Josh. "What about you?" she asked.

"I'm fine," Josh said. Just then the entire deck creaked alarmingly. "Come on, we'd better hurry up."

A few minutes later a second raft was bobbing in the water beside the first. "Ned, lie down on your stomach," Brooke instructed as Ned cautiously crept his way out onto it. "That way you can paddle with your hands. Ryan, Dani, and Angela, you guys push him along while you

swim. Josh, the twins, and I will take the supply raft."

The boat creaked again. As we were all heading for the edge of the boat, we heard another sound.

"Uuuuuuuh."

I paused with one leg over the side of the boat. "What was that?"

Brooke gasped, her hand flying to her mouth. "Mr. Truskey!"

When we rounded the cabin and the rear deck came into view, we saw that our teacher was leaning against the cabin's outside wall. He took a few woozy steps, almost tripping over his own feet. I couldn't believe we'd nearly forgotten all about him.

"Ah, there you are, Abigail," he said when Brooke skidded to a stop in front of him. "Did you bring the ice pack? I think I bumped my head."

"Just come on with me, Mr. Truskey," Brooke said soothingly. "We're going to get out of here now."

I exchanged a worried look with the twins. But there was no time to worry about Mr. Truskey at the moment. The boat let out yet another creak, and this time the deck shifted noticeably. It was time to get while the getting was still good.

Castaways

Macy and Ryan helped Brooke drag Mr. Truskey around to the front of the boat, where we all managed to get him onto the second raft. Ned wrinkled his nose as the teacher collapsed next to him and grabbed on to the sides of the raft. "Yuck," he said. "He smells like barf."

"Just hold on to him so he doesn't slide off," Brooke said firmly. "Now come on, everybody—let's go!"

The lagoon was a lot wider than it had looked from the deck of the boat. By the time our feet touched solid ground again, I was completely exhausted. My legs were rubbery, my arms felt like jelly, and my eyes ached from squinting against the bright sun reflecting off the water. We all staggered through the gentle surf, dragging both rafts up until they scraped against the bottom. Then we dumped Mr. Truskey out onto the wet sand. We left him there for a moment, letting the waves wash the rest of the vomit off him. But when an especially vigorous wave rolled over his face and he started to sputter, Brooke ordered Josh and Ned to drag him up beyond the waterline. Within seconds he was curled up in the sand, snoring happily.

Meanwhile the rest of us dragged the supply raft

beyond the reach of the waves. That pretty much finished us off. Even Brooke's order-spewing motormouth seemed worn out.

"Okay, everyone," she mumbled. "Five-minute break."

Quickly shrugging off my life vest, I collapsed on the beach beside the twins. The sand felt warm as it cradled my tired muscles, and I felt as if I could lie there forever, soaking up the rays and enjoying the pleasant tickle of the mild sea breeze.

Then I turned my head and saw that Angela had managed to position herself directly beside Josh on the sand. My jaw clenched, and suddenly I was no longer in the mood to relax. I sat up abruptly.

"So what now?" I demanded of the group at large.

Brooke rolled her head to the side just enough to look at me. "I guess we should make a plan or something," she said, though for once her heart didn't really seem to be into it.

I looked around at the members of our bedraggled little group. Mr. Truskey was still asleep, and Kenny was already chasing sand beetles a dozen yards down the beach. It looked as if Angela might have edged a little closer to Josh, though he had his eyes closed and seemed

unaware of her presence, which made me smirk just a little. Brooke, Ned, and the twins were also lying on the sand, while Ryan was on his knees poking at a clump of seaweed, and Macy was wringing the water out of the hem of her short-sleeved gingham blouse.

Josh opened his eyes and sat up. "Okay," he said. "So what's our plan?"

"I don't know," Brooke replied wearily. "I guess we should try to come up with some kind of signal to make it easier for our rescuers to find us. We could build a fire, or—"

"Wait," Macy interrupted with surprising conviction. "A signal is a good idea, but first things first. We don't know how long we're going to be stranded here. We need to be prepared, in case it's longer than we think."

Brooke rolled her eyes, but Josh was the first to speak. "Macy has a point," he said firmly. "Chances are someone will find us before sundown. But if they don't, we should be prepared."

"Josh is right," Angela said, putting a hand on Josh's arm.

"Fine, fine," Brooke said sourly. "I guess it wouldn't hurt to be prepared in case we're stuck here overnight or whatever. But let's not get too panicky about it."

I rubbed my aching arm muscles, wondering why she'd

insisted on dragging every plastic fork and can of soup off the boat if she was so sure we were going to be rescued right away. But I didn't bother to say anything about it. For one thing, I was pretty sure at that point that she was right. There was no way we were going to be stuck on that island for more than a day. Ms. Watson would make sure of that.

Ned raised his hand, looking worried. "I've been thinking," he said. "You know, we have no idea how far off course we are from where we're supposed to be. For all we know, we might've been going in the total wrong direction for like half an hour or more."

"What's your point?" Brooke asked.

"This Esparcir Island chain is huge," Ned said. "I read about it on the Internet—there are something like three hundred islands in it, stretching across miles and miles. And if we have no idea where we are, anyone looking for us isn't going to either. It could be days before we're found—maybe weeks!"

Five

A few hours later I was carrying an armful of branches out of the jungle when I tripped over something half-buried in the sand. The wood flew in all directions, and I had to windmill my arms frantically to keep from falling flat on my face.

"Darn it," I muttered when I regained my balance.

I kicked the sand away from whatever had tripped me. "What's that?" Chrissie panted, emerging from the tree-line with a small log under each arm. Her brow was beaded with sweat, and her curly hair was totally frizzed out in the humidity.

"Don't know." I kneeled down, brushing away the rest of the sand. My fingers touched a cool, hard surface that felt rough and smooth at the same time. "Oh," I said. "It's a shell."

"A big one!" Chrissie dropped her wood and peered at the shell.

I dug it the rest of the way out of the sand. It was a monster-sized conch, creamy pale but swirled with shades of pink. From end to spiraled end it had to be a good eighteen inches long. "I'd hate to see the snail that used to live in this thing," I joked, hoisting the shell in one hand for a better look. "It's kind of cool, isn't it?"

"Yeah." Chrissie already seemed to be losing interest in my discovery. She glanced over her shoulder. "So what do you think about this whole camp-building thing?"

I shrugged, following her gaze. A hundred yards down the beach, our pathetic little excuse for a camp was slowly taking shape. Brooke was standing near the small but growing heap of driftwood, fallen branches, and dried-up palm fronds that was supposed to become our campfire. The sun was setting over the horizon beyond the reef, sending pinkish streaks across the rippled surface of the lagoon. True to Josh's prediction, the remains

of our boat had sunk out of sight some time ago. None of us had even seen it go, probably because we were too busy acting as Brooke's personal servants.

"Brooke's a little out of control," I said. "But that's no big surprise—we already knew she was bossy. The worst part is watching Evil Angela morph into her right-hand girl."

"Tell me about it," Chrissie said with feeling. "Did you see the latest so-called job Brooke has her doing?"

I shifted the conch shell from one hand to the other, the feeling of its solid weight oddly satisfying. "I don't even want to know," I muttered.

She told me anyway. "She's stacking and arranging the cans of food on a ledge in one of the caves," she said, her dark eyes flashing at the injustice of it all. "We're stuck lugging firewood around, and poor Ned and Ryan have to dig a latrine in the jungle, while stupid Angela gets to sit around alphabetizing the vegetables."

I scratched the newest addition to my mosquito-bite collection. "Did you notice she's also managed to force Josh to stick around and keep her company?"

Chrissie shrugged, not seeming particularly interested in that aspect of Angela's evil plans. But it certainly hadn't escaped my attention. Earlier, while Angela was sup-

posed to be carrying the luggage up beyond the high-tide line, I'd noticed him helping her. Now I saw him standing beside the stack of supplies, handing her things one at a time. I gritted my teeth as I watched them for a moment. I seriously doubted it was Josh's idea to be her assistant. He was probably just too nice and polite to tell her to take a hike when she started ordering him around.

Suddenly noticing Brooke peering suspiciously in our direction, I dropped the conch shell back on the sand and started gathering up my firewood. "Come on," I said. "We'd better get moving before Queen Robinson Crusoe gives us a demerit."

When we reached the camp, we found most of the rest of the group already there. The only one missing was Mr. Truskey, who had awakened some time earlier and wandered off into the jungle. Almost everyone looked grimy, hot, and tired—Ned's face was bright red and streaked with dirt, the bow topping Macy's long ponytail was drooping, and I could feel an itchy trail of sweat trickling down my back under my T-shirt. Even Kenny was coated in mud and sand, though I suspected he'd spent more time chasing bugs and sand crabs than working. Angela and Brooke, of course, looked like they'd just spent the

afternoon at the beach. A real beach, I mean—the kind without any wood-gathering or latrine-digging.

"Good, you're here," Brooke said as Chrissie and I dropped our loads at the edge of the fire pile. "It's time for a progress meeting."

I collapsed on the sand. A progress meeting didn't sound that thrilling, but it had to be better than dragging buggy, splintery firewood out of the jungle.

For the next few minutes Brooke did her favorite thing: talk. And talk. And talk some more. She proudly explained how she had decided we should build our signal fire on the widest part of the beach, near the rocky cliffs I'd noticed earlier. That way, if rescuers didn't find us before sundown, we could spend the night in one of the caves that dotted the base of the cliffs. She'd even scoped out the biggest and best cave for that purpose.

"Why not just sleep on the beach?" Ryan called out.

Brooke smiled smugly. "Bad idea," she said. "It's the rainy season."

As one, we all glanced up at the sky. The sun was still drifting along on its orbit, trailing pink and orange ribbons of light. The sparse clouds were small, fluffy, and innocent-looking.

"How do you know that?" Chrissie asked suspiciously. "It only rained, like, once the whole time we were on the other island."

Brooke hesitated, and I saw her gaze wander toward Ned, who was hanging back on the outskirts of the group, fiddling with the dials on his portable radio. I immediately deduced that Ned had told Brooke about it being the rainy season. It was amazing how much obscure knowledge that guy had gathered from TV and the Internet.

I waited for her to acknowledge him. Instead she frowned at him. "Hey!" she said. "Are you getting any kind of signal on that thing?"

Ned shrugged, looking slightly guilty at being caught playing with his radio. "Just one station's coming in," he said. "It's been all salsa-type music so far—no news or anything."

"Well, give it here." Brooke held out her hand.

Ned stared at her. "Huh?"

"Give me the radio," Brooke said, sounding impatient. "Come on. We need to save the batteries for an emergency."

I wasn't sure what kind of emergency would require a quick dose of salsa music, but I kept quiet. If I started

complaining about Brooke's leadership decisions now, I wasn't sure I'd be able to stop. My stomach rumbled, and I glanced over at the cave where Angela had stacked the food.

"Hey," I said as Brooke tucked Ned's radio into her pocket. "When's dinner?"

"We'll deal with that in a minute," Brooke said. "First, is there any other business?"

"What do you mean?" Ryan asked blankly.

Brooke frowned. "You know," she said. "That's the part of the meeting where we figure out what else we need to talk about."

She sounded a little testy. I guessed she probably wished the rest of her student-council buddies were there on the island with her instead of us. To tell the truth, I was wishing pretty much the same thing.

Macy raised her hand. "What are we going to do about Mr. Truskey? He disappeared hours ago, and it's going to be dark soon."

"Hmm, good point." Brooke glanced toward the jungle, looking nervous. "Um, I guess maybe we should make up a search party or something? What do you all think?"

Nobody seemed eager to volunteer for that duty. We

debated it for a minute or two. Just as Josh was reluctantly volunteering to lead the rescue party, there was a sudden crashing sound from the jungle. A second later Mr. Truskey staggered into view, clutching a couple of hairy coconuts to his chest. His clothes were tattered and stained with mud, his hair resembled a squirrel's nest, and he'd lost a sandal. Again.

"Look what I found, people!" he announced, his eyes gleaming triumphantly. "Sustenance! The coconut gods have smiled upon us!"

"Um, where have you been, Mr. Truskey?" Brooke said. "We were worried about you."

Mr. Truskey didn't seem to hear her. "I will now lead you all in a coconut dance of thanks!" he cried enthusiastically. "Come on, everybody. Get on your feet!" He started jerking his limbs around randomly.

Ryan and Kenny jumped up immediately, shucking and jiving along with Mr. Truskey's weird dance moves. "Yay, coconuts!" Kenny yelled gleefully.

I rolled my eyes. Why did I have to get stuck with the most embarrassing little brother in the world?

After a moment Mr. Truskey abruptly stopped dancing and dropped the coconuts he was holding. "That was

great!" he cried. Without warning he collapsed onto the sand and started to snore. Angela hurried over and put her hand on his wrist, smugly pronouncing a moment later that his vital signs were strong. I still wasn't sure she knew what she was talking about, but there didn't seem to be much point in worrying about it just then. It wasn't like we could call 911 anyway.

The dancers sat down again, and we all stared at one another for a few minutes. When both Ned and Kenny started complaining that they were hungry, Brooke finally agreed that it was time to eat. She sent Ryan and Ned to fetch some of the food from the cave, and soon we were all chowing down. I'll tell you, I never would have thought cold canned beans could taste so good. I finished off a whole can on my own, with plenty of room left over for some slightly stale crackers. Still, as I watched Ned gulp down three cans of chili with hardly a pause for breath, I couldn't help worrying a little. There hadn't been all that much food on the boat, and it was already going fast. What if we were stuck here longer than we thought?

I did my best to shake off such thoughts as Cassie offered me a taste of her tomato soup. It wasn't as if I could do much about it anyway.

Worst Class Trip Ever

After we'd all eaten ourselves silly, we just sort of lazed around the firewood pile for a while, watching the sun sink lower in the sky. Now that Mr. Truskey was back and my stomach was full, things seemed a little brighter. The only thing still keeping me feeling down was the way Angela continued to hang all over Josh.

As I was trying to figure out how to wing a slimy wad of seaweed at her head without being caught, Kenny glanced up from playing with some kind of scuttling little beach-dwelling creature he'd found. I'm not sure what it was, but it had a lot of legs. "Hey," he said loudly. "I'm still thirsty. Where's the rest of the juice from the boat?"

"We need to save that for tomorrow morning," Brooke told him, muffling a small burp. "You'll have to drink water instead. Just go get some from that stream Ryan found earlier, okay?"

"Wait!" Macy said urgently as Kenny hopped to his feet. She cleared her throat. "Um, we'll have to wait until we get the fire going for that."

Brooke frowned. "What are you talking about?"

"She's right," Ned spoke up. "We have to boil the water before it'll be safe to drink."

I nodded, suddenly recalling seeing that on some kind

of wilderness TV show. "Yeah," I called out. "If we don't, we'll all end up with, like, brain parasites or something."

"Gross!" Angela wrinkled her nose and glared at me. "Dani, do you always have to be so disgusting?"

Meanwhile Brooke's expression wavered between confused, worried, and irritated. Finally, irritated won out. "Okay, whatever," she snapped. "Let's not waste any time, then. Ryan, go get some matches."

"They're on top of the stack of canned fruit on the left, behind the big greenish rock," Angela offered helpfully, though she didn't make a move to get up off her behind and help find them. After all, that would have meant moving more than eighteen inches away from Josh.

Ryan trotted off, disappearing through the entrance of the cave. It was dark and shadowy even a few feet inside, so we all lost sight of him for a moment.

Then there was a shout. "Whoa!" Ryan's voice cried, sounding weird and echoey.

"What is—," Brooke began, but her question ended in a shriek as, suddenly, a cloud of dark, flapping shapes burst out of the cave and swirled right toward us.

I yelped and leaped to my feet, almost crashing into several of the others as we all scurried to get out of the

way. Overhead I felt and heard the swoop of hundreds of wings beating the air. It felt as if the creatures were only inches above me, and I ducked my head, not quite daring to look up.

"Bats!" Kenny's delighted shout rang out above the screams, cries, and yelps. "Cool!"

It was all over in a moment. The bats dispersed to wherever bats go, disappearing into the twilight. Ryan emerged from the cave, a large box of wooden matches in one hand and a slightly dazed look on his face.

Slowly we all made our way back to the firewood pile. "That was freaky," Cassie said, her voice shaky. "I hate bats. No way am I sleeping in that cave tonight!"

"How can you hate bats?" her sister argued. "This is the first time you've ever seen one up close."

But her tone was subdued. Somehow I think Cassie's words had just brought home to all of us one very important fact—night was falling. It was going to be dark soon, and we were still on some unknown tropical island with no rescue party in sight. I shivered, the pleasant sea breeze suddenly feeling ominously cool. We had spent all afternoon talking about the possibility of spending the night on the island, but I'm not sure any of us really believed we

would actually have to do it. This wasn't like when we were younger and would spend all day setting up camp in the backyard, only to rush back inside to our warm, safe beds when the first spider crawled across the tent ceiling or a weird howl drifted out of the trees. This time we were stuck in that tent—no chickening out, no escape.

"Okay," Brooke said loudly. "Let's stop wasting time and get this fire lit."

That turned out not to be as easy as it seemed. For the next half hour, we all took turns holding lit matches to twigs and leaves and the edges of palm fronds, restacking the firewood and kindling, and arguing about the best way to do the first two things. It seemed to take forever before one of the tiny bits of flame actually grew, instead of flickering out. When it finally happened, we all cheered.

By the time the flames started crackling up and eating away at some of the larger branches, it was almost fully dark. A handful of stars flickered into view overhead, but a few new clouds had rolled in, obscuring the light of the moon, so that the cheerful orange glow of the fire was the only real source of light. I'm not normally afraid of the dark, but I was careful to keep my gaze on the flames, ignoring the weird-looking shadows dancing around in

the darkness at the edges of my vision. A cool breeze kicked up, turning my sweaty, sunburned skin cold and clammy.

Macy and Ryan took a large metal pot and a flashlight we'd brought from the boat and returned a few minutes later with a pot of water, which they set in the embers to boil. Then everyone huddled gratefully near the warmth of the flames. Even Brooke didn't have much to say for once. Kenny paced restlessly around the circle, then finally stopped right in front of me. "It's awfully dark out there, Dani," he mumbled, peering past me at the blackness beyond the fire's glow.

The panicky look in his eyes sent a shiver down my spine, but I did my best to hide that. I wasn't about to let the others think I was as big a chicken as my little brother. "Duh. That's what happens at night, twerp," I retorted irritably. "Now move out of my way—you're blocking the heat."

Kenny hesitated, staring from my face to the darkness and back again. When I scowled at him, he finally shuffled away. A few minutes later I noticed him sitting beside Macy, who had an arm around his shoulders. I also saw that Angela was cuddled up to Josh, her

blond head resting on his shoulder. He had both arms around his own knees and a slightly uncomfortable expression on his face, but I couldn't tell if the latter was due to Angela's presence or the overall situation.

I jumped as there was a sudden screech from the direction of the jungle. "Wh-what was that?" Cassie squeaked nervously.

"Probably just an owl or something," Brooke said, though she didn't sound as certain as she normally did about things. "They probably have owls here, right?"

Nobody answered her. My heart was pounding, and I forced myself to take a couple of deep breaths, using my basketball coach's favorite focusing technique to calm myself down. What was I so nervous about, anyway? We'd just spent four nights on an island very much like this one. So what was the big deal?

I shook my head, knowing that it wasn't the same thing at all. It was amazing how much louder the nighttime noises sounded out here. On the other island we'd had lights, a radio, real tents, and a couple of teachers to distract us, but here there was only the crackle of the fire to ward off the sounds.

Beside me, I noticed Cassie stifling a yawn. That set me

off, and I yawned so widely I was afraid my jaw would crack in two. All that swimming and wood-hauling was awfully tiring.

Soon everyone else was yawning too. "Okay," Josh said. "So where are we going to sleep?"

"I'm not going near that cave," Cassie said firmly.

Chrissie nodded her agreement. "It's warmer by the fire anyway. We can sleep right here."

"Good idea," Angela added, scooting even closer to Josh, if that was possible. "Those bats were sooo spooky!"

I glowered at her. She didn't notice, since she was too busy fluttering her eyelashes at Josh. She was really taking advantage of this chance to play girly-girl scared—I just hoped Josh saw through it.

Brooke shrugged, obviously not any more eager than the rest of us to head into the bat-infested cave. "Okay," she said. "Grab some palm fronds from the cave if you want something to sleep on. Girls on this side of the fire, guys over there on the other side of Mr. Truskey."

As we all shuffled around, shifting our positions according to Brooke's orders, Josh looked worried. "We should have brought the tents from the boat," he said. "Maybe we could rig up some kind of shelter out of the rafts—"

Castaways

"No!" Brooke said sharply. "That's a waste of time. Someone will be here to rescue us tomorrow. All we have to do is get through tonight."

I yawned, hoping she was right, but too tired to think about it much. Now that I wasn't hungry anymore, my sleepiness was quickly becoming overwhelming. I burrowed into the soft sand between the twins. It still retained some of the warmth from the sun and was surprisingly comfortable. Within moments I was drifting off to sleep to the soothing image of a luxury yacht arriving to rescue us the next morning, with just enough space on board for everyone except Angela. . . .

Crash!

I sat bolt upright an unknown amount of time later, every nerve ending quivering on alert. For a second I had no idea where I was. Then a jagged bolt of lightning bisected the sky immediately overhead, illuminating the sleepy-looking faces of the twins beside me, and it all came rushing back.

"What the . . . ," Cassie mumbled sleepily.

Another deafening clap of thunder swallowed the rest of her words. A second later the sky opened up with a drenching downpour.

Six

Within seconds the heavy rain doused the remains of the fire. "Come on!" I shouted hoarsely, leaping to my feet and grabbing a twin—I had no idea which one—by the arm. I felt the second twin grasp my other elbow, her fingernails digging into my skin. The rain was coming down so hard I could barely keep my eyes open, and my hair was plastered against my face, making it even harder to see. The three of us raced across the beach, aiming in what I hoped was the direction of the cliffs. If we accidentally went the other way and wound up in the surf, it would be hard to tell—we were already soaked to the skin.

I was vaguely aware of others running and shouting all around us, though it was hard to hear anything over the growling thunder and pounding rain.

"Got—to get—to the caves," I panted, though I doubted the twins could hear me.

In the next flash of lightning, I saw a small, dark hole in front of us in the base of the cliff. Gripping the twins tighter, I sprinted toward it.

A moment later we were inside. The sound of the rain was more muted once we were out of it, and the three of us collapsed in a heap on the stone-and-dirt floor. It was very dark, but the lightning flashing outside like fireworks illuminated things enough to see that the cave we were in was much smaller than the storage cave. In fact, it was barely bigger than the average bathroom stall back home. But it was a couple of feet above the level of the beach, and it was dry. I briefly wondered if there were bats hanging from the ceiling just a few feet above our heads, but I decided it was probably better not to think about that too much.

"Whew!" Chrissie panted, brushing a chunk of sopping-

wet hair out of her eyes. "This has got to be the worst thunderstorm I've ever seen!"

"No, it isn't," Cassie said. "That one last summer at camp was worse."

Chrissie shook her head. "Nuh-uh. Not even close."

I closed my eyes. The constant flash-dark-flash-dark was making my head hurt. "Come on," I said. "Let's get closer. I'm freezing!"

The three of us huddled together for warmth as the twins continued to argue. I sighed softly, almost wishing I'd ended up with someone else. Even Angela or Kenny seemed like an improvement . . .

Kenny. My eyes flew open again. I'd almost forgotten about my little brother. Had he found shelter? Was he still wandering out through that terrible storm some-where, scared and alone? Just then lightning flared over the beach, illuminating it as brightly as the noon-day sun, and I saw that there was nobody in sight out there.

Kenny would be fine, I told myself, banishing my worry. He'd probably suckered Macy or somebody into taking care of him.

Anyway, I had my own problems. I was wet and cold,

and the twins sounded like they were gearing up for a good, long argument.

Closing my eyes again, I nestled against Cassie's shoulder and did my best to ignore it all. I was sure I'd never be able to sleep again. . . .

I awakened to a bright, sunshiny day. The twins were still sleeping beside me, Chrissie with her mouth open and a dribble of drool trickling out of her mouth, and Cassie curled up like a puppy in the back corner of the cave.

When I sat up, my mouth felt dry and sticky and every muscle was sore and stiff. I squinted out at the beach. Near the remains of the fire Macy was bustling around doing something or other, while Brooke and Angela supervised Ryan and Kenny as they dragged more wood out of the jungle. Mr. Truskey appeared to be wading in the surf, wearing what looked like a long, black sock tied around his head like a bandanna.

Stretching and yawning, I stood up and hobbled out of the small cave. In the light of day, I could see that the twins and I had missed the main cave by just twenty yards or so. Glancing at the entrance to the larger cave, I wondered if the others had all found it. Had Angela and

Josh ended up in there together? Wrinkling my nose with disgust, I decided not to think about that anymore.

"Hey," Macy greeted me with a shy smile as I approached, glancing up from her task. Now I could see that she was pouring rainwater from various places where it had gathered—the large conch shell I'd found the day before, several empty food cans—into a big cooking pot we'd brought over from the boat.

"Can I help?" I asked, stifling another yawn. I picked up a can of water and carefully poured it into the pot.

"Thanks," Macy said. "I thought we'd better collect as much of this clean rainwater as we could. That way we won't have to boil any for a while." She glanced toward the fire pile. "It might take a while for the wood to dry out."

I glanced that way too, just in time to see Josh appear in the entrance to the large cave. He was carrying several cans and cartons of food.

"Is there any tomato sauce left?" Ryan called out to him.

"What's that all about?" I asked Macy, suddenly realizing that Ryan and Kenny were now crouched down beside another cooking pot.

"Brooke told Ryan and Kenny to fix breakfast for everyone," Macy replied, picking up a stray spoon with a

few drops of water in its bowl. "I think they're making some kind of cold potluck stew or something."

"Ick," I muttered. The last time Kenny tried to make his own breakfast, we almost had to call the fire department to put out the toaster. And Ryan was famous around school for eating anything and everything people had left over from their lunches—health food, doughnuts with the jelly licked out of them, French fries that had fallen on the floor.

By the time breakfast was ready, everyone was awake and hungry. I was pretty skeptical about eating anything that had been prepared by my little brother and Ryan, but I had to admit that their concoction tasted good. Everyone else seemed to agree, since every drop of the "stew" disappeared within five minutes flat. Even Mr. Truskey sounded almost normal as he complimented the two boys on their stew.

"You two should open your own breakfast restaurantaurus when we get back to Abu Dhabi," he added earnestly. "I'm sure it would go straight to number one on the *Billboard* charts."

Oh well. So much for normal.

As I licked some tomato sauce off my fingers, I noticed

Worst Class Trip Ever

Macy, who was sitting beside me, gazing worriedly at the pile of empty cans beside the wet firewood. She glanced over at Josh, who was sitting on her other side. "How much food is left in there?" she asked him quietly.

Josh shrugged. "We've gone through about a third of it so far," he said. "Maybe a little less."

"We should probably be more careful." Macy glanced out at the still water of the lagoon. "If we don't get rescued today . . ."

I shivered slightly at her words. We weren't exactly a bunch of seasoned survivalists. If we ran out of food before help arrived, would we be able to find a way to stay alive? How long could a middle-schooler survive without food, anyway?

Then I shook it off. Nobody else seemed too concerned, and Macy seemed to be a bit of a worrier by nature. Of course we would be rescued today. It wasn't as if Ms. Watson and the rescue party had to search the entire globe—just a few islands. With any luck we would be back home in Florida by dinnertime.

As Ned hopefully asked whether our breakfast included dessert, Mr. Truskey leaped to his feet. "I have a great idea for dessert, peoplesies!" he exclaimed.

Castaways

"Yesterday while expeditiationing, I spied the most lovely-dovely-looking red berries. . . ."

"Um, we probably shouldn't eat stuff if we don't know what it is, Mr. Truskey," Brooke pointed out. "It might, uh, make us sick or something."

"Nonsense!" Mr. Truskey patted his own belly. "Not with my cast-iron stomach."

I'm sure I wasn't the only one flashing back to the contents of his cast-iron stomach spraying all over the boat. But it didn't matter. Mr. Truskey strode off into the jungle, disappearing almost immediately into the thick, dripping undergrowth.

I shrugged, then swallowed a burp. Ms. Watson and the other rescuers could deal with him when they arrived. In the meantime my full stomach was telling me it was the perfect time for a nice, long nap in the shade.

We all spent the rest of the morning relaxing, working on our tans, playing in the surf, or exploring more of the island. After my nap I joined the twins on the beach until I could almost hear my skin sizzling in the tropical sun. Then I decided to leave them to their sunbathing and find some more sunscreen in the supply

cave—or better yet, find some shade.

I wandered across the beach and into the treeline at one end of the cliffs. After the blazing openness of the beach, it felt moist and cool and sort of private in there. Realizing it was the first time I'd been in the jungle when I wasn't busy looking for firewood or fetching water from the stream, I looked around with interest. Dapples of sunlight shivered across the shady jungle floor as the breeze rustled the treetops high overhead. Closer to the ground, layers of plant life dripped and waved and seemed to breathe out moisture. Brightly colored birds flickered along through the leaves, while numerous unseen insects droned lazily all around me.

And then, just as I was thinking how beautiful and peaceful and nice everything was, a huge choo-choo bug buzzed by. I swatted at it, just in case it was thinking of chomping on me.

"Get out, bugface," I muttered, waving my hand as the bug circled for another dive at me. "I mean it. Scram!"

"Talking to yourself?"

I spun around, forgetting all about the bug as I found myself staring into Josh's grinning face. "Um, I, uh, that is, er . . ." I stammered out a few more random syllables.

Then I swallowed hard, forcing myself to chill. Why did Josh Gallagher always seem to throw me off balance? "Choo-choo bug," I said succinctly.

"Ah." Josh nodded understandingly. "Yeah, I saw one just now too. Guess they're not as rare as Mr. Truskey thought. Remember, he told us there were hardly any outside of that other island."

"Uh-huh," I said intelligently. We strolled along together for a moment, following the rough path we'd all made through the jungle over the past day. Suddenly Josh stopped short and bent over, staring intently toward a particular bush.

"Pretty cool, huh?" he whispered, giving me a secret sort of smile.

At first I wasn't sure what he was talking about. The bush looked fairly boring to me—green leaves, green stems, the usual. Then I spied the butterfly gently fluttering on one of the branches, each panel of its gauzy wings like a tiny jewel.

"Yeah," I said softly, shivering a little as Josh's arm brushed mine. "Way cool."

I realized my heart was pounding kind of fast. Was it heatstroke, or was I suddenly changing like the Incredible

Hulk, morphing from regular old Dani McFeeney into some kind of swooning-over-boys, giggling-at-nothing, girly-girl creature? I shuddered again, this time at the thought of that. No way was I going to let some guy . . .

Suddenly I realized Josh was saying something again. "Huh—what?" I blurted out.

"I said, this whole trip will really be something to tell everyone about back home," Josh said. Either he was the politest guy in the world or the densest—there was no way he could miss the fact that I was behaving like some kind of drooling idiot who couldn't follow a simple conversation. But he just smiled normally at me as he continued. "I mean, it's not everyone who can say they were actually stranded on a deserted island, you know?"

I grinned. "Seriously," I agreed. As Josh and I walked on, pointing out other interesting sights to each other, I realized I was starting to settle down. Maybe even enjoy myself a little. When Josh's arm brushed against mine again, I didn't even pull it away.

Unfortunately, that didn't last long.

"Jo-o-osh!" Angela's sickly sweet, singsongy voice rang out through the jungle.

I gritted my teeth as she appeared at the end of the

path. "Oh, hey, Angela," Josh said pleasantly. "What's up?"

"Oh." Angela looked less than thrilled to find me with Josh. "There you are. Brooke says it's time to eat."

"Great," I said blandly, suddenly wishing I really was the Incredible Hulk. Maybe then I could do something about Evil Angela Barnes—and her terrible timing.

Our collective mood seemed to have dropped slightly by the time we'd all gathered around the fire area for lunch. The small amount of bug spray and sunscreen we had left was going fast, and the canned food was starting to look a lot less appetizing with each meal. As I picked at a can of peas, I found myself daydreaming about a double cheeseburger with extra pickles and a triple order of fries. Everybody else must have been having similar thoughts, because nobody had much to say.

At one point Macy tentatively suggested trying to get the fire going again, but nobody seemed very enthusiastic about that idea. The hot midday sun had burned off a lot of the puddles the rainstorm had left, but the remains of the fire still looked waterlogged and kind of depressing.

"Forget it," Brooke announced at last, the decisive tone

of her voice determined to put an end to the whole idea. "It's daytime, and it's hot. The last thing we need to do is waste our time and energy trying to start another fire."

As the afternoon wore on, we all grew progressively more bored and sunburned and cranky. The twins and I tried to get into some body surfing, but the waves were too small to make it much fun. Chrissie suggested swimming out to look at the coral formations of the reef, but that seemed like too much effort, and Cassie and I voted her down.

Eventually almost everyone drifted back to the fire area. Or rather, the nonfire area. Glancing around, I quickly counted heads. There was no sign of Mr. Truskey, and Kenny seemed to be missing too. Just as I was wondering if I should be worried about my little brother, he came running out of the jungle.

"Check it out, guys!" he shouted, sounding excited.

"What is it?" I snapped. "And where have you been? You shouldn't go wandering off by yourself like that, you loser."

His right hand was clenched into a fist. Ignoring my insult, he held it out to me and opened it. An enormous, ugly black beetle was sitting there.

"See?" he said, sounding as proud as if he'd just discovered the meaning of life. "It's a choo-choo bug!"

"Whoop-di-do," I said sourly, taking a step back. "I saw one earlier."

Kenny looked a little disappointed, but Ryan leaned forward with interest. "Hey," he said. "I thought those things only lived on that other island."

"Maybe that means we're closer to our original island than we thought!" Cassie exclaimed, her eyes lighting up. "We could've been going in circles out there on the water. That means we'll definitely be found as soon as they spot our smoke, and . . ."

Her voice drifted off, and everyone's gaze shifted to the fire site. Ned cleared his throat. "Um, not to point out the obvious or anything, but *what* smoke?"

"Don't be obnoxious." Brooke sounded more than a little defensive. "How was I supposed to know they'd take so freaking long to find us?"

"Never mind," Josh said, scratching at a bug bite on his leg. "The important thing now is to figure out what to do."

"Duh," Chrissie said, rolling her eyes. "The thing to do is build another fire. Ten hours ago." She glared at Brooke.

Brooke glared back. "Look, if you have something to say—"

"Listen to me."

I blinked in surprise, realizing that the firm, clear voice had come from Macy. Glancing over, I saw that she was climbing to her feet. Her old-fashioned clothes looked dirty and bedraggled, her nose and chin were bright pink with sunburn, and her long hair had leaves and twigs tangled in it. But her expression was determined and serious.

"What?" Brooke demanded sourly. "Are you going to tell me I'm a loser too?"

Macy didn't bother to answer. She looked around at all of us somberly. All of us looked back except for Kenny, who had wandered off to play with his choo-choo bug. "I've been thinking about this, and talking to Ned." She nodded at Ned, who smiled uncertainly. "We realized it might not even matter whether we have a signal fire or not."

"What are you talking about?" Ryan said.

"I'm sure you all read that information packet Mr. Truskey gave us before the trip, right?" Macy looked around expectantly.

I stared at my feet. Out of the corner of my eye, I could

tell that most of the others were doing the same. Apparently I wasn't the only one who'd decided there were more important things to do to get ready for the trip than reading some boring information packet— things like shopping for a new bathing suit, giving my parents the silent treatment for the Kenny Situation, and begging Michelle and Tina to change their minds and come along.

"Whatever," I said after a moment, breaking the guilty silence. "What about it?"

Macy shrugged. "Well, remember how the Esparcir chain is shaped sort of like a long, curvy bowling pin? Our original island was near the narrow end, close to the mainland. But there are tons and tons of islands at the farther, wider end. Also, a bunch of the islands through-out the chain have people living on them."

Ned nodded enthusiastically. "I looked some of them up on the Net," he put in. "The history of the tribes and stuff is really cool."

I gazed at him in surprise. I'd never really thought of Ned Campbell as the type to do spontaneous research on any topic more in-depth than TV trivia. In school he'd always seemed just as lazy mentally as he did physically.

"So get to the point," Angela told Macy impatiently. "Are you saying we should check the rest of this island to see if there's some stupid tribe living on it somewhere?"

"No." Macy answered her calmly, ignoring the sarcasm. "I'm sure we'd already know if that were the case. I'm just saying that we should be aware that a smoke signal might not mean that much—there are probably dozens or even hundreds of fires burning on different islands at all times."

My jaw dropped as what she'd just said sank in. All this time I'd been imagining Ms. Watson buzzing calmly along in a helicopter, spotting our fire, zipping down to the rescue. "She's right!" I blurted out. "We're totally hosed!"

Angela rolled her eyes. "Chill out, drama queen," she told me. "So they might have to check out a few false leads before they find us. No biggie if they get a helicopter or something."

"Won't work," Ned spoke up again. "You can't fly a helicopter over most of these islands—not safely anyway. There's this weird local wind pattern that makes it really dangerous. That's why we came out here in boats in the first place."

Things were sounding worse and worse. "So, what?" I

said, desperate to find a bright spot in all the bad news. "So they'll have to use boats to find us. All they need to do is spread out and check between our old island and the mainland."

"Right," Macy said. "*If* we're actually between the original island and the mainland."

"What are you talking about?" Brooke demanded. "Where else would we be? We couldn't have gone that far off course—and you're the one who said our island was at the narrow end of the bowling pin or whatever."

Macy glanced over at Ned. "Go ahead," she said. "Tell them what you told me."

Ned looked embarrassed. Clearing his throat, he awkwardly climbed to his feet. "Um, I noticed something weird yesterday on the boat," he began. "See, I was listening to my radio"—he paused long enough to glare at Brooke, obviously still nursing a grudge—"um, I was listening to a station from the mainland for a while. It was coming in pretty well at first, just like it did when we were on the old island. But the farther we went in the boat, the more staticky it got, until I could barely get it at all. I checked a few other stations, but nothing would come in except that salsa music."

Brooke looked blank. "So? What does that have to do with anything?"

Josh gasped. "Wait," he said. "Ned, dude, are you saying what I think you're saying?"

I guess the sunburn had affected my brain, because I still had no idea. Luckily Macy spoke up again, to spell it out for me.

"Mr. Truskey was already sick when we left the first island," she said grimly. "Probably a little delirious. It's quite possible we were going in the wrong direction the whole time—not just after he passed out. We could be miles and miles into the fat end of the bowling pin somewhere."

"And any search party would naturally be focused on the area between the original island and the mainland," Brooke said slowly, a look of horror dawning on her face.

I knew how she felt. "But they'll still find us," I said, trying to sound confident rather than desperate. "They'll definitely keep looking until they find us."

"Yeah," Josh said. "But if Ms. Watson misunderstood Mr. T and thinks we're waiting for her to get back with the second boat, she would only be getting there now and figuring out there's a problem."

There was an anxious murmur from the group. Now

that we were sitting down and putting the pieces together, things were sounding worse and worse.

"So you're saying they maybe haven't even started looking for us yet?" Cassie squealed.

Instead of answering, Josh pointed down the beach. "Hey, there's Mr. Truskey now."

The teacher wandered toward us. His shirt was so tattered that it was little more than strips of fabric, revealing his skinny, sunburned chest. Both of his sandals were gone, and his feet were black with dirt.

"Yikes," Ryan muttered. "He's not looking too good."

Cassie nodded, looking worried. "Shouldn't we do something about him?"

"Like what?" Brooke retorted. "Call an ambulance on our coconut phone? Weave a straitjacket out of palm fronds and check him into the island psycho ward?" She shrugged. "About all we can do is keep an eye on him and hope his choo-choo crazies don't get too much worse before we get rescued."

I winced, realizing she was right. Her comments also drove home the point that, like Mr. T's sanity, our immediate future was looking pretty strange and uncertain.

Mr. Truskey seemed quite cheerful as he reached the

fire area. "Hi there, people," he greeted us. "I hope you don't mind if I join you while I write in my journal?"

He held up a large, ragged piece of tree bark. Brooke stared at him anxiously. "Sure thing, Mr. Truskey," she said soothingly. "Why don't you have a seat right here with us?"

"Thank you, Beatrice." Instead of sitting, though, Mr. Truskey started wandering in a circle, scratching busily at the bark with a bit of shell. As far as I could tell, it wasn't actually making any marks on the "journal" at all.

"What are you writing, Mr. T?" I asked him.

He beamed at me. "I'm glad you asked, Ellie Mae," he said. "I'm composing an ode to the lesson equatootinal beachwookie beeble. It's in seventeen verses, all iambic pentameter." He put his shell-pen to his lip, staring out into space. "Now, what rhymes with 'thorax'?" he murmured thoughtfully.

We all stared at him as he turned and wandered off toward the jungle, still muttering to himself. Then we all stared at one another. It was pretty obvious that he wasn't going to be much help in figuring out what to do and how to survive on the island. That meant we were on our own until help came.

Whenever that was.

Seven

It only took a moment for Brooke to snap back into dictator mode. Jumping to her feet, she started barking orders.

"Josh, Ryan, Dani, start gathering some big branches and logs to build a shelter. Chrissie and Cassie, look for palm fronds to make a roof; and Ned, Macy, and Kenny, start bringing more firewood. I'll be in charge of arranging everything. Angela, go find the matches, and then see if you can make the life vests into a sort of mattress where the shelter will be."

I sighed. As usual, Angela got the cushy job while

everyone else was stuck with the grunt work.

"Wait," Cassie protested. "Shouldn't we talk about this first or something? Figure out what we want to do next, or—"

"Just shut up and do as I say," Brooke growled, a slight edge of panic in her voice. "Now! Now! And Chrissie, let Cassie deal with the palm fronds for now. You need to start gathering rocks so we can spell out S-O-S on the beach."

The twins and I exchanged a glance. The SOS thing didn't make much sense. For one thing, it would be dark in a few hours, so the shelter and fire seemed like higher priorities. Besides, we already knew our rescuers couldn't fly over the islands, so who was supposed to see the SOS?

But Brooke had a wild look in her eyes that made us all think better of arguing with her. "Okay, Brooke," Chrissie said mildly. "I'll get right on that."

"Maybe we can use the rocks to ring the fire pit," I whispered as we hurried away. "So at least it's not a total waste of time."

Half an hour later I was standing in the spot Brooke had proclaimed as the site of our shelter-to-be, swearing

under my breath. I was trying to figure out how to angle a trio of large, gnarled branches so they would hold each other up in a sort of tepee shape. It was hard, sweaty work—even though the sun was sinking toward the horizon again, the beach still felt like a sauna. Besides that, getting the branches to stand up wasn't turning out to be as easy as it had seemed at first. I was full of scratches from the tree branches falling on me, not to mention about a million new bites from the colony of ants I'd surprised in a log I'd found in the jungle.

Just as the branches collapsed for about the twenty-fifth time, one of them landing hard on my left foot, Angela wandered over from the storage cave. As I picked up two of the branches again, she stopped in front of me with her hands on her hips. "Stop wasting time, Daniel," she snotted. "It's not very fair to stand around out here while the boys are doing all the hard work for you out in the jungle."

Enough was enough. I was tempted to drop the largest branch right on her head. Instead I just threw it down with all my might. "THAT'S IT!" I yelled at the top of my lungs. *"I quit!"*

There was a moment of silence as everyone turned to stare. Angela goggled at me, clearly taken by surprise.

Brooke glanced at us from the fire area, then hurried over.

"What's the problem here?" she asked briskly. "Dani, why aren't you working on the shelter?"

"I was trying to," I whined, wiping sweat off my forehead with one hand. "But then Angela came over and started bugging me, and—"

Brooke rolled her eyes. "Grow up, Dani," she snapped. "We all need to work as a team if we want to pull things together here."

She might be the first runner-up to Angela in the Miss Obnoxious pageant, but she had a point. I almost backed down. Almost. The others were all watching by now, and I could see Josh staring at me in astonishment. My cheeks were flaming, and this time it had nothing to do with sunburn. I don't mind being the center of attention for something good, like making a three pointer on the basketball court or knowing the right answer in class, but I hate looking stupid in front of other people.

Then Angela opened her mouth again. "Thank you, Brooke," she began smugly. "I was just trying to tell her that we—"

Before she could finish, though, Ryan stepped forward. "No, Dani's right," he said, tossing down his own armful

of branches. "This is ridiculous. We're all running around, totally *loco*, without even knowing what we're doing. It's stupid."

As Brooke's jaw dropped in surprise, Josh stepped forward too. "Sorry, Brooke," he said diplomatically. "But he sort of has a point. Our camp is pathetic, and we need a better plan."

One by one, the others joined in the revolt. They were all sick of Brooke's bossy ways, and now that the mutiny had started, they were all more than willing to make their feelings known. I just watched in amazement as Ned, Macy, and the twins came to stand beside me, Ryan, and Josh. The only one missing was Kenny, who seemed unaware of the whole scene as he dumped another armful of kindling on the fire pile.

"Sorry, Brooke," I said, emboldened by all the support. "Looks like it might be time for some new ideas. Or maybe new leadership."

Brooke's fists were clenched so tightly at her sides that it looked like her knuckles could burst through her skin at any moment. "Fine," she said, her voice shaky. "Do whatever you want. I'm done."

She stomped away. "Brooke, wait!" Macy called. But

Worst Class Trip Ever

Brooke disappeared into one of the caves without looking back.

Angela glowered at us, saving her most evil glare for me. "Look what you've done," she said. "What are we supposed to do now?"

Ryan shrugged. "That's easy," he said. "We just need a new leader, like Dani said. I nominate Josh."

"Huh? What?" Josh looked startled. "No! That is, I don't think I'm the best person. Why don't you do it, Ry?"

"No way, he's too much of a spaz," Chrissie said. "I'll be the leader if you want."

Cassie snorted. "Yeah, right. You?"

"What's wrong with me?" Chrissie demanded.

"Forget it, she's right," Angela said. "If we need a new leader, *I'll* do it."

"Yeah, just what we need," I said sarcastically. "Instead of Brooke, we'll have Mini-Brooke."

"Wait!" Macy said. "Listen, I have an idea."

A week or two earlier, if Macy had spoken up like that during some equally heated argument in the school cafeteria, I doubt anyone would have heard her, let alone paid attention. But now everyone quieted down long enough to see what she had to say.

Castaways

When she had our attention, Macy looked a little uncomfortable. "Look," she said. "There's only one fair way to do this. We should take a vote."

Angela raised her hand. "An election? Okay," she said. "I nominate myself as a candidate for president of this island."

I rolled my eyes so hard I could practically see my own brain. How totally like Angela to keep nominating herself, especially right after her so-called friend Brooke had just been dethroned. So much for loyalty.

"Go on," Angela said. "Don't you guys know how this stuff works? Someone has to second the nomination to make it official."

She turned and glared meaningfully at Ryan. He sighed, then raised his hand weakly. "I second it."

"All right, that's one candidate," Macy said. "Who else wants to join in?"

I didn't notice that Kenny had wandered over to see what was going on until he spoke up. "I will!" he cried. "I nominate myself to be king of the island!"

I glared at him. "Very funny, half-wit," I said. "Now shut up and let the big kids finish their discussion."

Kenny scowled at me. "You shut up, Danielle," he exclaimed.

"Sorry, Ken," Macy said gently. "It's probably not a good idea for you to run as leader. But maybe you can be the assistant leader to whoever wins, okay?"

I rolled my eyes as Kenny smiled at her. That was just what he needed—someone feeding his fat little ego, not to mention his delusions of importance.

There was a long moment of silence. As the seconds ticked past and Angela's face looked increasingly smug, I felt my horror growing. This couldn't be happening—if we went from Brooke as our leader to Angela, it would be like flinging ourselves out of the frying pan right into a five-alarm wildfire. I had to do something.

"I nominate, um, Josh!" I said quickly.

Josh shook his head. "I already said I don't want to do it," he said. "If nobody wants the job except Angela, I think we should just let her do it."

"Thanks, Josh," Angela simpered. "I guess that means—"

"Me!" I blurted out. "I nominate myself!"

"Seconded," Cassie said.

"Thirded!" Chrissie added loyally.

Angela glared at me. I smiled back at her.

"Okay, then," I said pleasantly. "Looks like the race is on!"

Eight

I'll admit it. I couldn't help enjoying the look of pure rage on Angela's face. I had foiled her plans for world domination—well, island domination, anyway—and she knew it. There was no way she could beat me. The twins would definitely vote for me, and I was pretty sure that Macy and Ned liked me better than Angela. After all, I actually spoke to them like human beings once in a while. Then there was Kenny, who practically *had* to vote for me. Family loyalty and all that. And Josh . . . He wouldn't be stupid enough to vote for Angela, would he? I hoped she hadn't blinded him with her gooey smiles and poisonous attempts at flirting.

Then I shrugged, realizing it didn't matter. Even without Josh's vote, I still had it all wrapped up. There were only nine of us, not counting Brooke, so I just needed five votes to win, including my own.

"Well?" I said cheerfully, kicking my toe in the sand. "Should we take a vote right now?"

"No way," Angela retorted. "If we're going to do this, we should do it right."

"What do you mean?" Cassie asked.

Angela shrugged. "Well, you all know I'm a sixth-grade representative, right?"

I frowned. Her voice had suddenly turned syrupy sweet. That couldn't be a good sign.

"Get to the point, Barnes," I said sharply.

Angela shrugged. "I'm just saying, I know how these things work," she said calmly. "Elections, running things . . . I have more experience with that kind of stuff than anyone on the island except Brooke."

"Whatever," I said. "This isn't a bake sale or a pep rally we're talking about. So your experience doesn't mean diddly, okay? Let's just take a vote and get it over with."

A few people murmured, agreeing with me. I smiled,

almost tasting the victory. This just might make up for having Evil Angela along on this trip in the first place . . .

"Wait," Angela said, shattering my pleasant thoughts. "What about Brooke?"

"What about her?" I said.

Macy looked troubled. "No, she's right," she said. "Brooke should get a vote too. That's only fair."

"Yeah," Josh agreed. "In fact, if she wants to run against you guys . . ."

I wanted to snort with irritation. Wasn't the whole point of this election to find someone *other* than Brooke to lead us? I couldn't believe that Josh, of all people, was so concerned about being fair to our former tyrant.

Suddenly I thought of something that might change their minds. "But with Brooke voting, we're an even number," I pointed out. "What if there's a tie?"

Angela smirked. "Not feeling quite so confident now, McFeeney?"

"Hey, I can beat you at anything, anytime, anywhere," I retorted. "No question about it."

She took a step toward me, her hands on her hips and a menacing gleam in her blue eyes. "Is that so?"

"Look, guys," Josh broke in. He cast an anxious glance at

the sky, which was once again streaked with the pink and orange rays of the setting sun. "We don't have time to worry about this right now. How about if we pick up this election stuff tomorrow? Right now, we just need to get some kind of shelter thrown together in case it rains again."

"You're right," Macy said, and Ned and Ryan nodded.

"That's fine with me," Angela said. "We can campaign during the day and hold the election tomorrow night."

"Wait a second . . . ," I began, alarmed at the word *campaign*. Exactly what kind of sneaky, scheming vote grubbing did she have in mind anyway?

But the others were already moving on. "I think the best we can do right now is some kind of lean-to," Josh suggested. "Let's see if we can plant a couple of the bigger branches in the sand, then make the roof out of palm fronds. We can try to get something sturdier built tomorrow. Sound okay?"

The others nodded. "What about dinner?" Macy asked.

Josh glanced at the supply cave. "Maybe a couple of people can get started on that while the rest of us work on the shelter," he suggested. "Who feels like cooking?"

"I'll do it, if you want," Macy offered. She glanced at Kenny. "Want to help me, kiddo?"

Castaways

"Sure!" Kenny said. "I'm an expert cook, remember? I helped make breakfast, and nobody even got sick."

I rolled my eyes, but the others mostly laughed. "Good," Josh said. "Can you guys get the fire started, or do you need help with that? We'll need to boil some more water to drink."

"I can help them with the fire," Ryan spoke up. "Once it's going, I'll come help you guys."

Josh smiled. "Sounds like a plan. Let's go!"

By the time the sun disappeared into the ocean once again, we had a rough but functional shelter standing. We also had dinner waiting for us, though I was dismayed to find that Macy had decided to start rationing the food more carefully, which meant that we each only got about half a can's worth, plus a few crackers or potato chips.

"We can't be too careful," Macy explained. "Not when we don't have any idea how long we'll be stuck here."

"Good thinking, Macy," Josh agreed.

"Yes," Angela added quickly. "When I'm running things, one of the first things I plan to do is take inventory of our supplies and figure out the best and fairest way to use them and stuff."

Worst Class Trip Ever

Cassie poked me in the side. "Aren't you going to respond to that?" she hissed. "She's totally campaigning already!"

I bit my lip, realizing she was right. I couldn't let Angela get away with that, could I? The trouble was, I wasn't sure what I could say about our food supply that would be any different. For the first time, I really thought about what I was doing. Whoever won this vote was going to be responsible for the safety and well-being of the whole group for however long it took for us to be rescued. I like bossing people around as much as the next girl, but I wasn't sure I was ready for that kind of responsibility.

Then I shrugged. Whatever problems came up, I was sure I'd be able to handle them better than Miss Priss ever could. That was the important thing.

"I'll deal with that stuff tomorrow," I murmured to the twins. "I'm too tired right now. Unlike certain evil people around here, I did a lot of work today."

The next morning we all found Macy and Ryan up early preparing breakfast for everyone. "Ready to get this election started?" Angela asked, sounding suspiciously eager as she dipped into her portion of tuna-and-pea soup.

I met her gaze steadily. "I'm ready if you are," I replied.

Brooke looked up from her food. "What are you talking about?" she asked.

She had spent the entire previous evening sulking around the edges of the group. She hadn't even come into the shelter until the rest of us were almost asleep.

"We decided the fairest way to handle things would be to take a vote," Josh explained. "Angela and Dani both agreed to run for the position of leader."

"Them?" Brooke wrinkled her nose and stared at us like we were bugs in her soda. "But they're only *sixth* graders."

Josh shrugged. "We already agreed that if you'd like to put your name in the ring too—"

"Forget it," Brooke snapped before he could finish. "There's no way I want to lead you ungrateful bunch of losers anymore. I still get to vote though, right?"

"Of course, Brooke." Angela smiled her smarmiest smile at the older girl. "Your vote is totally important."

"Right, whatever," I said before the butt-kissing could go any further. "So why don't we just get this over with? We can take a vote right now."

Angela looked annoyed. "I thought we already decided to hold the vote tonight."

"No, *you* decided that," I reminded her.

"I was sort of thinking about that too," Josh put in. "At school we always do this kind of thing by secret ballot. Maybe we should do the same thing here." He cleared his throat. "You know . . . to avoid any hard feelings or whatever."

"But how?" Chrissie asked. "We don't have any paper or pencils or anything."

"I was thinking about that, too," Josh said. "Remember how Mr. Truskey was scratching on that bark with his shell?"

As a group we all glanced toward the supply cave. Mr. Truskey had turned up again around midnight, scaring us half to death by tripping over the corner of the shelter. Now he was crouched on the sand in the cave entrance, scribbling away on his so-called journal. The last I'd heard, he was composing a new ode, this one dedicated to the island's native screech owl.

"Um, I don't think he's actually writing anything," Cassie pointed out.

"No," Josh agreed. "But while we were gathering wood last night, I noticed there's some shale-type stuff down by the stream. I bet if we scratched on that with the right kind of rock, it would work pretty well—at least

well enough to write down someone's initial."

"Cool!" Ned seemed intrigued by the other boy's idea. "I can check it out today if you want—find the right kinds of rocks and stuff and make sure there are enough ballots for everyone."

"Excellent." Josh smiled at him, then widened it to include the rest of us. "What do you say? Is it a plan?"

"Okay, but what about the tie thing?" Chrissie spoke up. "With Brooke, we're even numbers."

Josh nodded. "I thought about that just before I fell asleep last night. At first I was thinking Mr. T could be the tiebreaker. But, um, that might not be such a great idea."

I had to agree with that. In his present state Mr. T was likely to nominate a choo-choo bug for leader.

"Good point," Macy said. "Maybe we should just draw straws or something if it's that close."

Josh nodded. "Exactly what I was thinking," he said. "So what do you guys think? Sound like a plan?"

"Sure," I said weakly, since everyone else was nodding, including Angela. The more this election situation evolved, the less I liked it. If we'd called an immediate, public vote last night, I knew I would've won easily. But

now? I didn't put it past Angela to snake her way into some extra votes somehow.

There wasn't much I could do about it at the moment without sounding as much like a whiny crybaby as Angela herself. I would just have to make certain that my votes were solid, and beat Angela at her own game.

By the time I finished my breakfast, I had it all figured out. I was starting off with at least five likely votes: my own, Cassie's, Chrissie's, Macy's, and Kenny's. Brooke would almost definitely vote for Angela, but even so, all I had to do was convince just one of the three boys to vote for me, and I was golden.

First, though, I wanted to make sure those five votes were solid. Most people had finished eating by then and hurried off in various directions. I soon spotted Kenny coming back from the direction of the latrine. I hurried over to him.

"Hey, squirt," I said, trying to make my voice friendly. "Just wanted to see how you're doing."

"Why?" He squinted up at me suspiciously, scratching at a bug bite on his butt. At least, I hoped that's why he was scratching.

Castaways

I sighed. So much for trying to talk to him like a normal person. "Look," I said. "I just want to make sure you're planning to vote for me. You'd better be, if you know what's good for you."

He smiled smugly. "Sorry," he said. "Angela already promised to make me her junior assistant leader if I vote for her instead."

I just goggled at him for a moment, stunned at the depths of Angela's evilness. I had been right to worry. My shock soon turned to deep, seething, boundless fury. How dare she try to turn my own flesh and blood against me!

Well, two could play at that game. If Angela could play dirty, so could I.

Nine

"Look," I told Kenny, thinking fast. No way was Evil Angela going to do this to me. No Way. "I don't care what she promised you. I'm your sister—I'm the one who has your best interests at heart, not her."

He didn't look impressed. I decided to change tactics.

"Okay," I said briskly. "What will it take to make you change your vote? Name your price."

Kenny blinked, looking confused. Before he could answer, Josh came jogging up to us. "Hi, Dani," he said. "How's it going?"

Castaways

"Um, okay," I said. I knew I should probably say something more, but my brain seemed to have stalled.

Josh turned to Kenny. "Hey, little dude." He gave him a friendly smack on the shoulder. "I'm going to try to do some fishing. Want to come?"

"Sure!" Kenny looked excited. "Maybe we can catch a shark."

Josh chuckled. "Hope not!" he said. "I want something we can eat. Those canned beans and stale crackers are getting really old." He shot me a sidelong glance. "Want to join us?"

I wished I could say yes. Hanging out with Josh—even with Kenny along—definitely sounded like more fun than trying to convince a bunch of people to vote for me. But a girl has to do what a girl has to do. And what I had to do right then was make sure I humiliated Angela that night at the vote.

"Not right now," I told Josh reluctantly. "Maybe later."

Josh shrugged. "Okay. Come on, Ken. Let's go."

I watched them head down toward the water, then stomped off in the opposite direction. So far, my campaign was off to a spectacularly lame start. I had to change that—fast.

Worst Class Trip Ever

I was so focused on my own thoughts that I almost tripped over Brooke, who was lying on the beach in her bathing suit. Her head was resting on a life vest, and her eyes were closed as she soaked up the sun.

She opened her eyes and looked up at me. "What?" she said lazily, shading her eyes.

"Nothing," I said. "Don't let me disturb you."

Her eyes drifted closed again, and she wriggled slightly to adjust her position on the warm sand. It was obvious she wasn't planning to work too hard at anything now that she wasn't our leader anymore. It was even more obvious that I would be wasting my time trying to win her vote. After all, I was the one who was sort of responsible for her ouster, and I was sure she wouldn't forget that. Brooke definitely struck me as someone who could hold a grudge.

In the water nearby, Ryan and the twins were body surfing. The waves weren't very big, but the three of them seemed to be having a great time. As I watched, Chrissie sneaked up behind Ryan, who was looking over his shoulder for the next wave, and splashed him. He shouted in surprise, then swept his arm over the surface of the lagoon, sending a sheet of water cascading over her. She

shrieked with laughter, calling to her twin to come and save her. Soon a full-fledged water fight was under way.

"Okay, looks like they're a little busy," I muttered to myself, absentmindedly waving one hand in front of my face as a choo-choo bug buzzed past. I wasn't worried about the twins of course, but Ryan was one of my possible swing votes. I wanted to lock him in before Angela got to him and confused him with her big blue eyes and girly-girl shtick. Still, I figured I could work on that later.

My gaze wandered back toward Josh. He'd brought his own collapsible fishing pole on the trip. I remembered seeing him using it back on the other island. He hadn't caught anything then as far as I knew, but he looked like he knew what he was doing as he showed Kenny how to cast and then reel the line back in.

I noticed Ned sitting on the beach, watching the fishing lesson. "Aha," I muttered. "My first victim."

Ned squinted up at me as I approached. He was wearing only his bathing suit, and his shoulders were bright pink with a fresh layer of sunburn. "Hi, Dani," he said, reaching around to scratch one of the many bug bites on his broad back.

"Hey, Ned." I made my voice as friendly and sincere as possible. "What's going on?"

He glanced out toward the water. "Do you think those guys will catch any fish?"

I shrugged. "Josh probably will, if Kenny doesn't get in his way too much." Realizing that the best way to Ned's vote was through his stomach, I added, "It would be nice to have more to eat, huh?"

"Yeah." Ned rubbed his stomach absently, his gaze wandering from Josh and Kenny over to Ryan and the twins. "I'd kill for a bag of Doritos right now."

"Well, then you should definitely vote for me tonight, okay?" I said. "Because I have lots of great ideas about ways for us to eat better until we're rescued."

At that, Ned turned his attention from the body surfers back to me for a moment. He looked curious, though not quite as thrilled, overwhelmed, and grateful as I'd hoped. "Really? Like what?"

"Um . . ." I stared blankly out toward Josh, who was making another cast. The truth was, I hadn't thought much about the food situation at all. I figured I'd have plenty of time for that sort of thing once I was elected. "Too many things to name," I said at last. "But trust me—you'll eat

way better with me than you would with Angela."

"But what do you—," he began.

I decided it was time for a quick change of subject. "Hey, but you don't have to take my word for it," I said brightly. "I'll prove it to you—I'll let you have half of my lunch ration today. How does that sound?"

"Good," he said hungrily. "But I still don't know who I'm going to vote for."

"What if I give you three-quarters of my lunch?" I offered, feeling slightly desperate. Somehow, this wasn't going quite as well as I'd imagined. Ned was so passive— I'd figured all I had to do was *tell* him to vote for me, and he would.

He shrugged and scratched at another bite, grunting slightly as he tried to stretch his arm farther around his shoulder. "Sorry. I can't promise anything."

I could tell I was losing his attention. He stared out toward Ryan and the twins, who appeared to be playing freeze tag in the water. I searched my mind for another angle. "Look," I said. "I know you were really bummed when Brooke grabbed your radio."

"Yeah?" he said cautiously, still scratching.

"If you vote me in as your leader, I'm not going to be

anywhere near that bossy and unfair," I said. "Not like Angela, who was just like Brooke's evil henchman anyway. As my first move as group leader, I promise I'd give you your radio back."

"Really?" He thought about that for a moment. "Okay. I'll take that into consideration when I make up my mind."

I bit back a sigh. Obviously he wasn't in any hurry to make a decision, even with his radio or food on the line. What could be more important than that stuff to someone like him?

I peered at him out of the corner of my eye, trying to figure out a new angle. Once again he was staring out at the trio playing in the water. For the first time I noticed that he had an odd expression on his face—intent and sort of . . . wistful?

My mind started chugging along, putting the pieces together. I stared out at the twins with their curly hair, their pretty, exotic faces, and their perky personalities. It was no secret that lots of guys at school had big crushes on them. Could it be . . . ?

Ned absently twisted around to scratch at his bug bites again. "Ow," he muttered, wincing. He rubbed gingerly at the spot he'd just scratched, shooting me a sheepish glance.

"Stupid sunburn. I keep scratching too hard by mistake."

Suddenly an idea popped into my head fully formed. "Listen," I said, trying to hide my eagerness. "Forget lunch and all that. I have an even better idea."

Ned sighed. "What?" he said dully, his gaze already wandering back toward the twins.

"If you agree to vote for me tonight, here's what I'll do for you," I told him. "I'll get my, er, campaign managers, Chrissie and Cassie, to be your personal scratchers for the day. They'll hang out with you as much as you want and take care of those pesky, hard-to-reach itchy bug bites. And I'll make sure they're extra-careful not to hurt your sunburn."

Even as I blurted it out, the idea started to sound a little goofy. I winced, for once sort of understanding why my parents were always chiding me about not thinking before I spoke. But then I saw that Ned looked cautiously interested.

"Really?" he said. "Um, the twins would do that?"

I gulped, realizing I had no idea if they would or not. But how could they say no to helping me out? That was what friends were for. Besides, I knew they didn't want Angela to win any more than I did. Anything for the cause . . .

"Totally," I assured Ned. "So what do you say?"

Ned's eyes were practically glowing. "Okay," he blurted out, suddenly sounding shy and a little uncertain. "I'll do it. I'll vote for you."

"Excellent!" I crowed. *Take that, Angela,* I added silently. I smiled at Ned. "I'll be right back with your back scratchers."

That was three votes locked up, plus my own of course. All I needed was two more to win, and I was pretty sure I had at least one of them already. . . .

As I splashed into the surf I glanced around for Macy, but she was nowhere in sight. My eyes narrowed as I realized the only other person missing was Angela. Were the two of them together? Was Angela trying to bring her over to the dark side?

There was no time to worry about that at the moment. I headed for the twins.

"What?" Chrissie said in disbelief when I explained the situation. "You're kidding, right?"

Cassie shuddered. "Ew," she said. "There's no way I'm touching Ned Campbell's skeevy back. Not even with a fifty-foot pole."

"But that was the only way I could get Ned to vote for

me," I said. "Please, you have to help me out on this."

Chrissie rolled her eyes and splashed toward shore. "Um, I beg to differ. We totally *don't* have to."

Cassie and I followed her out of the water and onto the sand. I glanced down the beach at Ned, who was staring at us hopefully. "You guys don't want Angela to win, do you?" I said, feeling a little desperate. "Think of the torture of having her as a leader."

Cassie wrinkled her nose at me. "I'm busy thinking of the torture of spending all day rubbing Ned's buggy back," she declared. "I mean, for all we know, we could end up getting rescued tonight. So it would all be for nothing anyway, and it wouldn't even matter who wins the stupid election."

"Good point, Cass," Chrissie agreed.

I bit my lip. Of all the times for them to be in perfect agreement!

"Come on," I pleaded. "If I go back and say no now, he'll be totally crushed and humiliated. Plus he'll think you guys are snobs or something." I could tell right away from the looks on their faces that maybe that wasn't the angle I should've taken. "Er, I mean, he'll think I'm a total flake," I amended quickly.

"That's your problem," Chrissie said flatly.

I was opening my mouth to keep arguing when I heard someone hurrying up behind us. Glancing over my shoulder, I saw that it was Josh.

"Catch anything?" Cassie asked him, way too obviously relieved at the chance to change the subject.

"Not yet," Josh admitted. "What are you guys looking so serious about over here?"

Chrissie smirked at me. "Dani's very concerned about Ned's itchy back."

I glared at her. The last thing I wanted was for Josh to find out about my stupid offer. "That's right," I put in quickly, before she could reveal anything more. "He's really itchy, and he can't reach very well to scratch the bug bites on his back, and when he tries, it hurts the sunburned spots. I'm just worried about him."

"That's nice of you, Dani." Josh looked thoughtful. "Listen, if you want some help, I think I have an idea. . . ."

I watched, embarrassed and a little confused, as he hurried up the beach toward the forest line. "Thanks a lot, you guys," I hissed at the twins. "Way to make me look like an idiot."

They just smirked. "You're welcome," Chrissie said.

Castaways

Josh returned, holding a sturdy, gnarled tree branch about two feet long. "Now, if I can just find one of those sea sponge things Ken was showing me...," he murmured.

A few minutes later I dragged myself back over to Ned, holding behind my back the scratcher thingy Josh had created. How in the world was I supposed to spin this?

"Well?" he said when I reached him.

"Sorry," I muttered, staring at the ground, the trees, the sky—anywhere but his round, hopeful eyes. "Um, I kind of need the twins for, uh, campaigning and stuff. But we came up with an even better solution."

Ned stared at the back scratcher as I whipped it out. "What's that?"

I demonstrated how it worked. "See?" I said, trying to sound cheerful. "Now you don't have the hassle of telling someone where it itches. You can do it yourself! It's long enough to reach all the itchy spots, and the sea sponge is rough enough to scratch your bites but soft enough not to bother your sunburn."

"Oh," Ned said flatly. His eyes went dark and sort of gloomy as he took the back scratcher from me and stared at it. "I get it."

I bit my lip. It was obvious that he was disappointed, not to mention humiliated. He had to realize the true reason I couldn't come through with my promise—he might be lazy, but he wasn't stupid. "Sorry," I began, feeling terrible—and not just because I could almost see his vote slipping away. "I hope you don't—"

"Ned! There you are!"

I spun around to see Angela approaching. "What are *you* doing here?" I muttered.

"Josh just told me how much Ned's back is bothering him," she said sweetly. "I thought I'd come over and try to help."

She stepped closer, fluttering her eyelashes, and smiling as she plucked the back scratcher out of Ned's hand. "Wha-what . . . ," he mumbled.

"Now, just hold still and let me take care of these nasty old bites," she cooed, going to work with the back scratcher.

She wasn't exactly offering to touch him with her own fingers or anything, but judging by the slightly awed expression on his face, I suspected such details were lost on him. He was probably already composing

the story about this he would tell his buddies in the AV club when he got home. Miss Perfect, Angela Barnes, practically hanging all over him . . .

I gritted my teeth, furious with her—and with myself for messing up so badly. Angela was better than I'd thought. Much better. I was going to have to step up my game big-time if I wanted to win tonight.

And I *was* going to win. No matter what.

Ten

An hour later I was walking

Macy to the latrine, trying to get her to swear she was going to vote for me. Who knew that would be so difficult, considering the options? For some reason, though, she was uncomfortable with the idea of swearing on the lives of all her living relatives and pets.

Just then I spotted Angela and Ryan over near the supply cave. I stopped short, trying to hear what they were saying. I couldn't make out their words, but I could hear Angela's stupid little tinkling laugh and see her toss her blond hair over her shoulder.

Castaways

"Um, Dani? I'll see you later, okay?" Macy said. Without waiting for an answer, she scooted off toward the latrine.

I hardly noticed. I was too busy staring at Angela with barely contained fury. Did she really think she could win over all the boys just by flirting outrageously with them? Her silky blond hair and perfect manicure might win her more attention than she deserved back home, but on the island it wasn't going to cut it. At least, I hoped not.

I hurried over. "Excuse me," I said loudly.

She turned and glared at me. "There's no excuse for you," she snapped.

"Very mature, Barnes," I said before turning to Ryan with a friendly smile. "Hey, what's up? I wanted to talk to you."

"Do you mind?" Angela glared at me. "We were trying to have a private conversation here before you so rudely interrupted."

"Trying to make up for lost time, huh?" I said. "Think about it, Ryan. Did Angela ever want to talk to you before? Did she ever even give you the time of day until this election came along?"

Ryan shrugged, looking uncomfortable. "I dunno," he mumbled. "I just, you know, I want to help out. I mean,

I have some ideas about stuff we could do, you know, like to find more food or whatever, and—"

"That's cool, Ryan," Angela said smoothly. "And that's exactly why I was just telling you I'm the best candidate for the job. I'm used to working with lots of different people with different ideas, like on the Tweedale Student Council, and—"

"Yeah, yeah, yeah." I rolled my eyes. "Like the Tweedale Student Council ever has to worry about stuff like which berries are edible and which will kill you, or how long you have to boil the water so it doesn't give you the Truskey crazies. At least be honest with people—being on student council doesn't have anything to do with being a good leader on this island, and you know it."

"What does someone like you know about leadership, anyway?" Angela huffed. "Being a good leader isn't just about being honest or whatever. It's also stuff like figuring out who you can count on to help out, or being patient with spazzy people who think they know more than they do—"

"Oh, you mean like poor Ryan here?" I jerked a thumb toward Ryan. "Nice way to insult one of your possible voters, oh great superleader." I snorted. "I mean, at least

I can talk to people about the vote without letting them know I think they're losers."

"Hey," Ryan protested weakly.

Realizing I might have just accidentally insulted him, I smiled quickly. "No offense, dude," I added.

"Oh, yeah?" Angela countered snottily, ignoring Ryan completely. "You mean like the way you insult Kenny every chance you get?"

I clenched my hands at my sides. "That's different, and you know it," I said tightly. "What I say to my bratty little troll of a brother is none of your . . ."

The rest of my words were drowned out by a whoop from the direction of the shore. Glancing over, I saw Josh running up the beach, waving something in one hand and looking excited. Kenny was dancing on the sand nearby, waving his arms over his head, while Brooke and the twins hurried down from the caves to see what was going on.

"Hey, looks like Josh caught a fish!" Ryan said. "Think I'll go check it out."

"Ryan, wait!" Angela and I said at the same time.

But it was too late. He was gone.

144

Worst Class Trip Ever

"Look, let me put this in a way you can understand," I told Kenny, calling upon every ounce of patience I possessed to *not* add "you idiotic little nose picker." I stared over his head toward the water, where Ryan was fishing with Josh's pole. Josh himself was nowhere in sight. Too bad— he was next on my list. If anyone had the sense to see things my way, it would be Josh. He was way too smart to fall for Angela's ridiculous electioneering.

Kenny sighed so loudly that a light spray of spittle flew out from his lips and onto my arm, bringing my attention back to him. Gross.

"I know, I know," he said wearily, kicking at the base of a palm tree. "You already told me a million times. Angela didn't mean what she told me, blah-blah-blah."

"But I don't think you're really *hearing* me," I insisted. "Think about it. Why would she pick some runt like you as her junior assistant leader? I mean, *nobody* would do that, let alone a two-faced snob like Angela Barnes."

While I was talking, Kenny reached into his pocket, pulling out a handful of weird-looking purplish worms, the latest of the many creepy or disgusting species he'd already befriended on the new island. He held the worms up to his face and stared at them, seeming much

more interested in their vigorous wriggling than in what I was saying.

"Put those things away," I said irritably, slapping at his hands. "Are you really too dim to realize how important this is?"

Kenny snatched the worms away before I could knock them out of his hand. "Quit it," he whined, tucking his slimy little pets back in the pocket of his shorts. "Angela's right. You *are* way too mean to me."

"Oh, please," I said. "I mean, you're talking about trusting our survival on this island to a person who's so shallow she thinks choosing the right lip gloss is a majorly earth-shattering decision, and all you can do is—"

"Telling lies about me again, Dani?"

I spun around to see Angela's smirky face right behind me. "Eavesdropping again, Angela?" I countered. "That's not very nice."

"Neither is insulting your sweet little brother." Angela shot Kenny a sickeningly sugary smile. "You can always come to me if she's giving you a hard time, Kenny."

"That's low, even for you, Barnes," I snarled. "I mean, come on. Trying to turn my own brother against me?"

She shrugged. "I don't need to try," she said. "You do all

the work yourself by being so mean to him all the time."

"Yeah," Kenny put in.

"Shut up, twerp," I growled at him. "Angela's just suck-ing up to you because she can't get any votes from the mature people on this island."

"Are you including yourself in that group, Dani?" Angela said. "Because if so, I'm afraid you're pathetically mis-taken. You're even less mature than your little brother."

"What?" Kenny protested. "I thought you said I was very mature for my age."

Angela shot him a smile, though it looked kind of forced. "Oh, you are," she assured him. "It's just that your age is, you know, pretty low. It's not like you're in middle school like the rest of us, or—"

Kenny scowled. "I get it," he snapped. "You think I'm some stupid baby who's too young to be on this trip. Just like *her*." He jerked a thumb in my direction. "Well, I might be younger than you guys, but I'm old enough to know one thing: The worms in my pocket would make a better leader than either of you!" He spun on his heel and stomped away.

"See what you did?" Angela said accusingly as he dis-appeared into the woods.

My jaw dropped. "What *I* did?" I exclaimed. "*You're* the one who practically called him an infant."

"Maybe so, but he wouldn't be so freaking sensitive if you weren't always—" Suddenly she cut herself off, glancing over my left shoulder. "Hi there, guys!" she called, her voice and expression all sweetness and light again.

Following her glance, I saw Josh, Brooke, and Macy emerging from the forest nearby. All three of them were wearing wide smiles and carrying armfuls of something.

"Check it out, you guys!" Josh called. "We found a grove of fruit trees—see?" He held up one of the items he was carrying, which looked sort of like a large, yellowish avocado.

Brooke nodded. "Macy's almost positive they're papayas," she added happily. "That means no more of that disgusting canned junk. It's fresh fruit for us from now on!"

"Great," I said weakly as they dumped their harvest on the sand. "Um, Josh, could I talk to you for a minute?"

"No, *I* need to talk to you first, Josh," Angela said quickly.

Josh brushed off his hands on his shorts. "Later, okay?" he said, sounding distracted. "We're going back to get more fruit."

Worst Class Trip Ever

"Excuse me! Could I have your attention please, everyone?"

I glanced up at Angela from my snack of ripe papaya; she had just climbed atop a big rock near the fire pit. The fruit the others had brought back from the jungle was sitting in a pile nearby. The whole group was gathered around the fire pit, sampling the papayas. Well, everyone except Mr. Truskey. The only sign of him since breakfast was the faint sound of someone singing "Jingle Bells" from somewhere in the jungle.

Macy was the only one not eating. She was busy trying to scrape the scales off of several fish with one of the butter knives we'd brought from the boat. It didn't look like it was working very well; she kept muttering under her breath and tossing her head to keep her hair out of her face.

"What's that jerk Angela up to now?" I muttered to the twins, who were sitting next to me, eagerly scooping the last bits of ripe pulp out of their papaya skin.

"Mmuh, kuh," Chrissie mumbled with her mouth full, seeming disinterested.

Cassie looked over at Macy with concern. "Do you think she's going to be able to get those fish cleaned?" she whispered to her twin. "I'm starved, but I don't want to eat fish scales. They might be poisonous."

"They're not poisonous," Chrissie replied. "Now be quiet—Angela's trying to say something."

The twins looked up at Angela. By now, everyone else was staring at her too.

"Thank you so much," she cooed. "I just wanted to take this opportunity to say a few words before the vote this evening. . . ."

A campaign speech! She was giving a freaking campaign speech. Why hadn't I thought of that?

She started blabbing about how wonderful she was. ". . . And I have lots of ideas for ways to get food," she said smoothly. She waved one hand at the pile of papayas. "Like more fruit like this—"

I couldn't take it anymore. "Oh, yeah?" I called out loudly. "You mean that fruit that *other people* found while you were trying to trick people into voting for you?"

Cassie shot me a shocked look. "Dani!" she exclaimed.

"Well, it's true," I insisted. "She's spent the whole day lying about all the great stuff she's going to do while she lets you guys do the work of keeping this camp going."

Angela put her hands on her hips and glared at me.

"Oh, yeah?" she said. "I haven't exactly seen *you* working your fingers to the bone today either."

Kenny giggled. "Dani hates chores," he said through a mouthful of papaya. "Mom and Dad say she's the laziest daughter they have."

"That's different," I snapped at Angela, ignoring my little brother. "I'm busy trying to tell people the truth, so they don't make a horrible mistake."

"Oh, please." Angela rolled her eyes, her lips pursed into a sour-lemon look.

Out of the corner of my eye I noticed Josh staring at me in surprise, which made my cheeks suddenly feel a little hot beneath my sunburn. But I couldn't stop now. Not when I was so close to revealing Angela as the fraud she was.

"Don't have a response for that, do you?" I taunted her. "No wonder. You can't deny you're just a big fake."

"Not," she retorted. "Anyway, at least I'm not a big-mouthed know-it-all like you."

"Snob," I snapped.

"Loser," Angela shot back.

"Wuss."

Castaways

"Freak."

"Goody-goody—"

Somewhere in a little side room of my consciousness, I was vaguely aware that Mr. Truskey had just turned up again and joined the group at the fire pit. He seemed totally unaware of our argument as he wandered toward Macy and peered over her shoulder at the fish. After a moment he pulled a pocketknife out of the tattered remains of his shorts and handed it to Macy. Looking excited, she immediately opened it and set to work with new energy.

I gritted my teeth when I noticed that everyone else suddenly seemed more interested in the whole fish situation than in my argument with Angela. That's what I got for trying to talk sense to them before lunch.

But I wasn't giving up. I was going to convince them I was right about Evil Angela Barnes if it was the last thing I did.

Eleven

Sometime during the afternoon Kenny managed to catch a little green-and-yellow tree frog. He decided to keep it in one of the empty cracker boxes from the supply cave, with holes punched in the top for air. After that, anytime he walked by, I could hear a little *thump, thump, thump* as the frog jumped around inside the box.

My stomach hopped and flipped nervously, feeling just like that tree frog as I glanced out at the reef. The lower rim of the setting sun was just touching the top of the highest chunk of coral. It was almost time for the vote.

Castaways

I glanced wildly around the beach, feeling helpless and agitated. Thanks to Evil Angela's shenanigans, I still wasn't sure I had the votes I needed to win. And I *needed* to win. If Angela beat me . . .

A shudder ran through my body. I couldn't let that happen. No way.

The twins were perched together on one of the logs Ryan and Ned had dragged out of the jungle and set in a semicircle around the fire pit. Speaking of the fire, it was crackling away merrily again, adding its cheerful orangey glow to the streaky pinkish colors of the sunset. The tantalizing scent of cooking fish drifted across the beach on the gentle sea breeze, as Macy and Kenny tended Josh and Ryan's catch on the spit that someone had made out of branches. Brooke and Angela were sitting on the logs near the twins, while Josh, Ned, and Ryan sprawled on the warm sand nearby. As usual Mr. Truskey was nowhere in sight.

I joined the twins, sitting down on the next log. "Hi there," I greeted them cheerily.

They glanced warily at me. "What?" Chrissie demanded.

"What do you mean, 'what'?" I frowned at them. "Can't a girl come say hi to her friends?"

"'Hi', yes," Chrissie replied. "'Angela-is-dumb-so-vote-for-me-and-here's-a-million-stupid-reasons-why', not so much."

"Fine," I said, feeling slightly wounded. "I thought you cared about this election. I thought you cared about the battle between good and evil on this island. Maybe I was wrong."

Cassie rolled her eyes. "Melodramatic much?" she murmured, just barely loud enough for me to hear.

I glared at her, tempted to remind her that she was the one whose picture was probably in the dictionary next to the word *melodramatic*.

But I kept quiet. I couldn't afford to antagonize her, not now. All I could do was hope that she got over her annoyance before the vote. I looked around the fire, ready to do some last-minute campaigning. But after a moment I realized that nobody would meet my eye. When I glanced over at Ryan, he quickly stared down, suddenly totally fascinated with some kind of microscopic creature crawling along the sand in front of him. Ned was staring fixedly up at the sunset like it was the season finale of his favorite show. Every time my gaze wandered toward Macy, her own gaze was clamped firmly onto the sizzling fish.

Castaways

My only comfort was glancing over just in time to see Brooke roll her eyes at something Angela had just said to her, and stomp away toward the supply cave. Angela looked up and caught me smirking. She shot me a glare, then hurried after Brooke.

Before she could catch her, Josh stood up and clapped his hands. Everyone stopped what they were doing and looked at him expectantly.

"Hey, guys," he said. "Ready to do this?"

Brooke drifted back toward the fire as Angela took her seat again, smoothing out the legs of her shorts. Ryan and Ned sat up and moved in a little closer. Everyone remained silent as Josh held up a box filled with chunks of slate and bits of shell and explained how to mark them for our votes. Then he handed the box to Kenny, who eagerly took it and started passing out the voting supplies.

I found myself shivering, and it wasn't from the cooling evening air. This was it. It was time. Soon the suspense would be ended, and I would know my fate. What if Angela *did* beat me? How would I deal with the humiliation?

Then another thought occurred to me. What if she

didn't beat me? What if I won—and became the leader of our little tribe? What then?

I bit my lower lip, realizing I hadn't thought much beyond the election. Sure, I'd made promises about things I would do once I was leader, like find more food or build a better shelter. But I hadn't really thought about actually being in charge, being responsible for all of us until help came. Suddenly I wasn't sure which would be worse—winning or losing.

"Okay," Josh called as Kenny finished handing out the slates. "Everybody ready? Let's vote. Remember, all you need to do is scratch in the initial of the person you want to be our leader. *A* for Angela, or *D* for Dani."

I quickly scrawled a big *D* on my shale, then stood up and hurried forward to drop it into the box. It landed there with a satisfying *clunk*. Everyone else was still bent over their bits of shale as I returned to my spot.

Sitting back down, I scratched at a bug bite and glanced around the circle, doing a quick mental count. Even though the twins seemed kind of annoyed with me, I was pretty sure there was no way they would vote for Angela. So that was three sure votes, including my own.

Unfortunately those were the only ones I could be sure

of. I was afraid Ned might still be holding a grudge against me for that back-scratcher thing. I also couldn't help remembering that when I'd tried to apologize to Ryan for my inadvertent "loser" crack earlier, I'd accidentally called him hyper and crazy. Then there was Macy. I still thought she probably preferred me to Angela, but it was a little hard to tell. The last six or seven times I'd tried to talk to her about the issues, she'd ended up making an excuse and running away.

Angela stood up and carried her vote over to the box. Bending down, she dropped her piece of shale in carefully, then spun on her heel. She tossed her hair, and gave me a snooty, self-satisfied glance as she pranced past. I kept my expression calm and neutral, not wanting to give her the satisfaction of a response to her ridiculous behavior.

Hours, days, and eons seemed to pass as, one by one, the others got up and dropped their votes into the box. Brooke and Josh were the next ones finished after Angela, followed by Kenny, Ryan, Macy, Ned, and the twins.

Finally Josh stood up. "Okay, I think that's everyone," he said. "Who wants to count up the votes?" When no one seemed in any hurry to volunteer, he shrugged. "All right, guess I'll do it."

He walked over and picked up the box, carrying it back to his place by the fire. I kept my eyes focused on it, afraid to look anywhere else.

Setting the box on the ground by his feet, Josh looked up and smiled at me and Angela in turn. "Good luck to both of you," he said sincerely. "May the best person win."

"Thanks, Josh," Angela said in her syrupy-sweetest voice.

"Yeah," I added quickly. "Thanks." *And now hurry up and count the votes!* I added silently, just wanting the whole thing to be over.

Josh fished a piece of shale out of the box. He held it up and squinted at it. The sun was almost gone now, and it was getting pretty dark on the beach outside the ring of light cast by the fire.

"Okay," he said. "Looks like the first vote is *A* for Angela."

My heart stopped for a second. I swear it did—stopped dead. As Josh held up the vote for everyone to see, I squinted at it. There was a little smiley face drawn in the middle part of the *A*.

I rolled my eyes as my heart started pumping again. That had to be Angela's own vote for herself. A quick glance over at her revealed that she looked nervous rather than smirky and superior, which pretty much confirmed that this was just her own self-vote.

I held my breath as Josh pulled another vote out of the box. He peered at it. "That's another one," he said. "Two votes for Angela."

Uh-oh. This time I didn't dare look her way. If she won, I would be seeing plenty of her smug face soon enough.

I also didn't dare look at anyone else. Was this supposed to be telling me something? For the first time I wondered if I might have gone a little overboard in my campaigning. A few people had seemed a little annoyed—like the twins, for instance. And Macy. And Ryan. And Ned . . . Oh well, too late now.

Josh already had the next vote in his hand. "It's a D," he said. "That's one for Dani."

He held it up, and I tried not to look too eager as I leaned forward to see. It definitely wasn't my own vote—the D looked smaller and neater than the one I'd written. Whew! At least I hadn't alienated everyone. It would be bad enough to lose to Angela. But to lose in a blowout? If that had happened, I would've had to crawl off into the jungle to live in solitary humiliation among the choo-choo bugs. Maybe at least they would elect me their queen.

"Next vote looks like a . . . huh?" Josh brought the piece of shale so close to his face that he almost poked himself in the eye. "I—I can't make this one out," he admitted. "It doesn't look like an *A or* a *D.*"

"Let me see." Kenny leaned over and grabbed it. "You're right," he announced after a second, twisting and turning the shale this way and that. "It looks more like a *C.* Or maybe a *J,* if you hold it this way."

There was silence around the fire as all of us stared at Josh. He took back the vote from Kenny, glanced at it again, and shrugged. "Oh well," he said. "I'll just put this one aside for now. I guess we'll come back to it later if the vote is close enough for it to matter."

As he fished for the next bit of shale, I sat back and tried to take a few deep breaths. The suspense was killing me. Josh seemed to take forever fishing around for the next piece of shale, and in the meantime I sort of drifted back into my little fantasy about becoming Dani McFeeney, Queen of Bugs. I could see it now: My buggy minions would banish the other humans from the island, or maybe enslave them to help pick a never-ending supply of papayas for me. The choo-choo bugs would create elaborate dances and skits to entertain

me, while fanning me with palm fronds. . . .

"Dani," Josh said.

"Huh?" I blurted, snapping out of my thoughts of being carried aloft in glory by millions of my fanatically loyal choo-choo-bug subjects. "What did you say?"

There were a few giggles from around the circle. But Josh just smiled patiently. "I said that's another vote for you. See?"

He held up another piece of shale. This time I recognized the writing. It was my own vote.

"That makes it two-two, a tie vote so far between Dani and Angela," Josh said, sounding like some kind of sportscaster. "Plus that one mystery vote for *C* or *J* or whatever."

He leaned forward. I held my breath.

"The next vote is"—Josh held up the piece of shale, and a look of surprise crossed his face—"another *J*?" He shook his head, turning the vote this way and that, as if that would suddenly shake it into a letter that made more sense. "Oo-kay," he murmured.

"Check the next one," Brooke suggested, sounding strangely eager. "See what it says."

Josh shrugged and grabbed another vote. "It's a *J* too," he said, already reaching into the box for the next one.

He sounded increasingly perplexed. At least I wasn't the only one. "So's this one. And this one, and the last one too."

Suddenly Kenny let out a shout of laughter. "I get it!" he crowed. "It's like a write-in candidate. Everyone voted for Josh!"

Twelve

There was a moment of noisy chaos as we all realized that Kenny was right. Finally Brooke stood up and waved her arms over her head.

"Quiet!" she shouted. "Listen up, people. I'll admit it—I voted for Josh." She glanced around the circle, for a moment looking a little more like her old, smug self. "Now I know I'm not the only one who was getting totally sick of the two real candidates." She paused to shoot dirty looks at me and Angela. "I thought Josh would make a much better leader than either of them, so I wrote him down."

Worst Class Trip Ever

She sat down again. There was a long moment of dead silence. Nobody else seemed willing to own up the way Brooke just had. But nobody was exactly denying it either. I glanced over at Angela, who looked just about as flummoxed as I felt. Feeling my face slowly turning about twenty-three shades of red, I realized it was true—Josh had beaten both of us, his six votes to two for each of us.

When I shifted my gaze over to Josh, he looked astonished. "But—but I didn't even volunteer to run! Why would you all pick me?"

Even in my stunned state of mind, I realized that Josh hadn't voted for himself. He wasn't the type to do something like that, and besides, he just looked way too surprised. So who had he voted for? Angela and I had each received one other vote. . . .

I forgot about that as Angela spoke up. "That's just fine, Josh," she said, the sickly-sweet tone she always used while talking to him sounding a little bit sour around the edges. "I'm sure you'll do a wonderful job as leader."

Josh held out both his hands, his dark eyes alarmed. "But I don't want to be the leader!" he protested. "Seriously, we should really just take another vote or something—"

Castaways

"No way," Brooke said. "Why should we have to vote for one of these two"—she waved a dismissive hand toward Angela and me—"when you're the one who's been doing the most work?"

"That's a good point." Cassie shot a slightly nervous glance at Angela, then at me. "I mean, Josh was totally the one who helped us all get off the boat safely after the wreck."

Ryan nodded vigorously. "He had all the big ideas about how to build those rafts," he agreed. "I just helped."

"And don't forget the fish." Ned pointed to the fish still roasting over the fire.

"Plus he went out and found that papaya grove," Chrissie added.

The others all spoke up at once, babbling enthusiastically about how much Josh was doing around camp. At first I couldn't help feeling irritated and insulted. Here I was, volunteering to take responsibility for leading the way, and all they could talk about was Josh, Josh, Josh!

But the more I heard, the more it dawned on me that they were right. While Angela and I had spent the past twenty-four hours thinking only about how to get ourselves elected, Josh had been thinking about the camp.

He'd found lots of ways to make life on the island a little more comfortable for everyone.

It was true. He really was the most incredible guy I'd ever met.

I was a little embarrassed to realize I was staring at him. Luckily he didn't notice, since everyone else was looking at him too. He was still trying to turn down the job as leader. But as the others continued to harass and cajole him, he finally held up both hands in a gesture of surrender.

"All right, all right," he said loudly, struggling to be heard over the babble of other voices. "I guess I'll do it, if you all really insist."

The others cheered. All I could do was sit there and smile weakly, wondering if I would ever recover from this humiliation. The only bright spot was that when I sneaked a peek at Angela, she looked like she was even more freaked out than I was.

"But there's one condition," Josh continued when the cheers died down. "I'll only be the leader if both Angela and Dani will agree to be, like, my co-vice-leaders." He turned and smiled at the two of us expectantly. "Well?"

I returned his smile feebly, then glanced over at

Castaways

Angela. As soon as I saw that familiar little smirk cross her face, I opened my mouth to turn down the job. It was embarrassing enough to get stuck being vice-leader to the guy who'd beaten me out for the top job. But how could anyone expect me to share the position with Evil Angela Barnes?

Then something else occurred to me. What if I turned it down but she accepted? Just about the only thing I could imagine being worse than working with Angela was watching her have an excuse to drool all over Josh even more than she was already doing.

"Fine," I blurted out. "I'll do it."

Angela glared at me. "Me too," she said through clenched teeth. "I'm in."

"Cool!" Josh looked relieved. "That's great. Isn't it, guys?"

He glanced around at the others, who obediently cheered again. I noticed they sounded slightly less enthusiastic this time, but I figured I should take what I could get.

"Thanks, I—," I began.

"Thank you, everyone!" Angela interrupted loudly, standing up and placing one hand over her heart. What a drama queen. "I promise to do my best to fulfill this

duty, to help Josh as he works to serve the needs of all of you. . . ."

There was more, but I was rolling my eyes too hard to listen. Oh yeah. *This* was going to be fun.

The next morning the three of us held our first official meeting. We started by talking about ways to improve our camp, like building a better shelter and digging more latrines, and then moved on to ideas for gathering food.

"And I think we should split everyone into teams," Josh said earnestly. "With maybe two or three people on each. That way, one team can fish while another gathers firewood or whatever. And everyone will know what they need to do to keep the camp running."

"Sounds great. But we should rotate the jobs too," Angela suggested. "Like, one day team A is on water duty, but the next day team B does that while team A takes care of the fire or whatever. That way nobody gets bored or feels like they're doing more work than anyone else, you know?"

I forced myself to smile. "Good idea, Angela," I said pleasantly. Her comment really did make a lot of sense,

but it still just about killed me to give her any kind of compliment.

"Thanks, Dani," she responded, her tone just as polite as mine.

"No problem," I said. It wasn't easy to avoid adding "priss face" at the end, but I managed. The last thing I was going to do was let Angela make me look petty or immature in front of Josh. "Maybe we should pick the teams by drawing straws or something, so it's completely fair."

As Josh and Angela briefly debated my idea, I kept quiet and watched them curiously for a moment. A lot had changed over the past three days since our boat hit that coral reef, and not only in the state of everyone's personal hygiene. I was starting to see some of the people on this trip a little differently than I used to—most definitely including Josh. I'd always thought he was nice, smart, cute, and a good basketball player. But now that I was getting a chance to know him better, I realized he was even more interesting and special than I'd thought. Maybe more interesting and special than anyone else I'd ever known. What did that mean? And more importantly, did he have any of the same kinds of feelings about me?

Josh turned his smile toward me. "What do you think,

Dani?" he asked. "Should we just have everyone draw names out of a hat?"

"Um—sure," I said. "Sounds fair." Was it my imagination, or was his smile a little brighter when he looked at me than when he looked at Angela?

Imagination. Definitely my imagination, I told myself, not wanting to get myself all worked up over nothing.

Or *was* it nothing? Ever since last night, my mind kept returning to the vote. Once I'd gotten over the humiliation aspect of it, my curiosity took over and refused to let go. There had been one extra vote for me and one for Angela, and one of those had obviously come from Josh. Had he voted for me—or for her?

I chewed my lower lip, running over the maybes and what-ifs in my mind for the millionth time. Brooke had voted for Josh, which meant she couldn't have been Angela's second vote. Who else might have voted for the Evil One? Ryan or Ned? She'd flirted like crazy with both of them—if either of them had voted for her, that meant Josh had to have voted for me. Then again, it was quite possible that Kenny or Macy had voted for me, which would mean Josh had voted for Angela. . . .

Shaking my head, I tried to banish such thoughts. All

they did was tumble through my mind, over and over, without ever telling me anything for sure. What good did that do? Besides, why should I care so much whether Josh had voted for me or not? That was so totally the type of thing someone like Angela herself would worry about. *I* wasn't like that. No way.

"Hey, look," Josh said, pointing down the beach. "Mr. T's back."

Sure enough the teacher had just emerged from the jungle, looking sweatier and more disheveled than ever. His sunburned skin was starting to peel, his bark "journal" was hanging around his neck by a piece of twine, and he appeared to be muttering intently to himself as he wandered in a zigzag line toward the water's edge.

As I watched him splash into the shallows, a sudden flurry of movement back at the supply cave caught my eye. "What are Kenny and Ned doing?" I gasped as the flash of sunlight on aluminum answered my question. "Hey!" I blurted out. "They're snitching extra cans of food!"

"I think we need to work out a rationing plan for the supplies we have left," Angela said grimly. "Otherwise everything will be gone way too soon."

Worst Class Trip Ever

To my surprise I found myself nodding in agreement. But Josh bit his lip, looking worried.

"That can wait a little while, I think," he said. "First, we'd better get everyone started collecting firewood. Otherwise we won't have enough to keep the fire going through the day, and we'll need it to boil more water."

He was right. The firewood pile was down to almost nothing, and the fire was burning pretty low already. My stomach clenched with anxiety as I realized it was time to forget about that silly election and focus on more important things. Food. Fire. Water. Shelter. Basically, surviving until help arrived.

Whenever that might be.

The End . . .
for now . . .

star power

by Catherine Hapka

She's beautiful, she's talented, she's famous.

She's a star!

Things would be perfect
if only her family
was around to help
her celebrate. . . .

Follow the
adventures of
fourteen-year-old
pop star
Star Calloway